Dervishes' Inn

Dream Accounts of the Truth Seekers

Khalid Sohail

Rabia Al Raba

Translation: Naeem Ashraf

2019

Copyright

Published in 2019 by Green Zone Publishing

A division of Dr. Sohail MPC Inc.

213 Byron St. South

Whitby, Ontario Canada L1N 4P7

T. 905-666-7253   F. 905-666-4397

E-mail: welcome@drsohail.com

Website: www.drsohail.com

Dervishes' Inn

Khalid Sohail, 1952 –

Rabia Al Raba, 1974 -

Naeem Ashraf, 1964 -

    1.   Letter Fiction   2. Philosophy

ISBN – 978-1-927874-32-5

Cover Design   Shahid Shafiq

Textual Design   Marcelina Naini

Special thanks to

Shahid Shafiq for artistic cover

Marcelina Naini for formatting the book

and Anne Henderson for her creative suggestions

Dedicated to

The seekers of truth

Dervish can be a saint, sadhu, Sufi, scholar, mystic, artist, scientist, a common man or a woman who is in search of truth

Dream and Reality

Dervishes' Inn was a dream. Mr. Wajahat Masood, through his Hum Sub internet platform, turned this dream into reality. A few words of gratitude won't be able to do justice to his magnanimous gesture. Rather any words of thanks might tarnish the color of this beautiful reality.

We can only wish that all his dreams come true.

The Door

"O Dervish! Why do you keep telling your pupils, 'Do not lose hope, keep knocking, the door will open one day'. Did you not know that the door was never closed?"

- Rabia Basri

Atheist Saints

The religious geniuses of all ages have been distinguished by this kind of religious feeling, which knows no dogma and no God conceive in man's image; so that there can be no church whose central teachings are based on it. Hence it is precisely among the heretics of every age that we find men who were filled with this highest kind of religious feeling and where in many cases regarded by their contemporaries as atheists, sometimes also as saints.

- Albert Einstein

	Contents	
Date	*Title of the Dream*	*Page*
	Prologue	

Prologue

Naeem Ashraf – Translator

The foundations of all contemporary knowledge and collective wisdom held by humanity were laid on ancient translations. Anthropologists claim that what we know today was translated by someone somewhere centuries ago. In Urdu literature, translations occupy a substantial space as we see fiction and poetry translated from Greek, French, Chinese, German, Russian, English, Persian, Sanskrit and Hindi. Translations break language barriers and in a way transfer the cultures. But unfortunately translators are not given due place on the canvas of literary arts.

Translating a piece of literature from a local language to a global language is like digging a link-canal to connect a smaller river to a deeper and wider one. The translator must have a good knowledge of both languages including the vocabulary, idioms and phrases, just as civil engineer must have a sound knowledge of soil, the lay of the land and construction techniques before digging a link-canal. I do not claim a mastery over the Urdu and English. However, I have some experience translating over a hundred Urdu short stories into English. These are contained in three books namely: *Trespass'*, *Cliché and Sweetheart*. *Trespass* has already been published by *Sang e Meel Publications Lahore in 2016* and the other two books are under publication in Ireland and Pakistan respectively. *Dervishes' Inn* would be my fourth milestone. I have enjoyed this the most.

I took five months to translate these letters. They have been written in third-person format where Dervish and Rabia are two characters of the story cum creative discourse. Dervish is a poet, writer, psychotherapist and a scholar. Secular and liberal he lives in the West, whereas, Rabia is an Eastern woman with an established name in

Urdu story writing. She is intellectually liberal and to some extent secular but accepts Eastern tradition more by default than by design. Impressed by the Islamic mythological character Rabia Basri, Rabia has an affection for Prophet Yousef of Abrahamic lineage. The two co-writers have divergent views about man-woman relationships, friendship, psyche, spirituality and religion. Dervish always follows a scientific approach to resolve the problems of life, whereas Rabia takes a spiritual and religious line to highlight the issues related to Eastern culture. The contrast of opposing worldviews is what makes the discourse interesting and colorful.

The genre of letter fiction in Urdu literature can be traced back to *Ghalib Kay Khatoot or Makateebe Ghalib* but these were published as monologues. The letters of Allama Iqbal to Atya Faizi were published but again as one-way traffic. Letter writing does occupy a significant space in Urdu Literature but mostly we see collections of monologues. Any literary exchange or two-way traffic of more than a dozen letters is nonexistent in Urdu, at least in the past hundred years. We may say that unfortunately a beautiful genre of Urdu Literature has been buried under the dust of literary history. The revolution in information technology has also tarnished the very flavor of letter writing.

In such an atmosphere, reviving letter writing and revitalizing Letter Fiction is no less than revamping the entire literary culture and creating history. These letters which the authors call *Dream Accounts* are a great venture and perhaps the only Urdu literary project of the 21st century. Both writers have candidly spoken their respective truths about religion, history, literature, love, sex, marriage, friendship, man-woman relationships, psychology and spiritualty.

My five-month-long journey of translation was aimed at connecting the footprints of two creative travelers to build an easy trail for truth seekers across the globe. It commenced in November last year and ended in April this year. I travelled across diverse lands of Eastern and Western culture — mountains of research, jungles of knowledge, deserts of solitude and rivers of wisdom. When I got tired, I partook of the slumber of beautiful poetry to refresh and replenish myself travel. My march was hard in the beginning but became smooth after crossing a few hills of disorientation, as Rabia on her way had often swayed between the conscious and subconscious mind. Then there were days when I thought Rabia had lost the direction, so I had to bring her back through my map of translation and compass of articulation. Dervish who was the leader in the journey always kept moving. Upon covering a certain distance, he would sit on the high ground of affection and smile at me. I would forget my weariness time and take the next leap.

Towards the end of the journey Dervish took me to a cottage of nostalgia on an isolated canal bank of mother's love. There Dervish handed me the precious gifts of two poems "Mother Earth is Sad" and "Aging Eyes". They revived and encouraged me to finish the journey. During the last leg of my march I remained under the spell of both poems especially "Aging Eyes". The destination was nearing. I was now speedily scaling the cliffs of transformation. I enjoyed the clarity of mind and flow of thoughts coming from Dervish especially Green Zone philosophy, and the connection of creativity, insanity, and spirituality. The essence of true beauty, friendship and deep love changed my worldview about these important aspects of life. Such relevant yet delicate explorations make this book not just a bedtime book but worthy of a serious read.

I feel indebted to Rabia for introducing me to Dr. Khalid Sohail who brought about a healthy and creative change in my literary life. Thank-you, Rabia.

I find no adequate words to thank Dr. Khalid Sohail for affording me an opportunity not only to translate a historical book of letter fiction but also to get it published in Canada. He is a living example of what Bertrand Russell calls the "best life". In his words, "The best life is always inspired by love and driven by knowledge". *Dervishes Inn* is another feather in his cap.

Through this humble effort of translation this creative, meaningful and thought-provoking dialogue will now be available to an English readership across the globe. I wish more writers, poets, artists, philosophers and scholars would make pen friends and embark upon healthy discourse by writing such philosophical, creative and literary letters.

Happy reading!

First Dream

The First Step towards Friendship

30th April 2018

Respected Miss Rabia,

First, I wish to extend my heartiest gratitude to you for having read my creations and sending me a friend request on Facebook. I am also grateful to you for having asked for my short stories along with my picture for inclusion in your upcoming short story anthology.

Now I want to make a literary confession.

When I look back over my past years exploring the literary world, I came across two kinds of writers, scholars and intellectuals. The first group includes those with whom dialogue is possible. If dialogue is possible then friendship too is a possibility. With the second group, dialogue is not possible which implies that friendship too is a remote possibility. However, a two-way monologue can take place between me and the people who belong to the second group. But unfortunately, monologues are like two banks of a river. Since a bridge of communication cannot be built over the banks of monologues, an estrangement exists despite numerous interactions.

After having read your short stories, I realized that a debate can ensue between us. And if debate is possible, then hopefully friendship might also find a place. In short, your stories motivated me to start a correspondence with you, to embark upon homework that might pave the way for dialogue and friendship. If you were in Toronto, I would have invited you to dinner and dialogue. I do it for my local and foreign friends. My friends are my precious assets; they inspire me, and I take pride in their friendship.

Having read your Afsanas, [short stories], my first impression is that you are well-versed in the psyche of modern man and woman. You know the intricacies of multifaceted relations between men and women, yet while expressing the notions of love you do not include to metaphors of sin or reward. That is the most impressive aspect of your stories. Reading your Afsanas was a treat, indeed a pleasant surprise for me. I wonder how you acquired such a delicate consciousness, awareness and insight. I have been living in Toronto for quite some time, as a psychotherapist, it is understandable that I learnt the agonies and pleasures of human relations through my patients, friends and foes here in a foreign land. But how you learnt all that, I can't believe...

The psychological aspects of romantic discourses between man and woman have been creatively depicted in your stories, "Sweetheart" and "Camouflage". These two stories relate romantic discourses with social aspects. You have boldly painted the romantic bond of a man / woman with the vibrant colors of life. This is a fictional miracle and I am impressed with it. I congratulate you on writing such wonderful pieces of fiction.

Like other evils, our writers too have peer-rivalry. They amply criticize as critics, but when it comes to appreciating a genuine work, they display a dearth of positive words. Most critics hold works of fiction up to religious or cultural mirrors. They forget that the fine arts have no religious, cultural or geographical boundaries, rather they have their own criteria to measure strength in any piece of fiction....

Your Afsana not only contains the psyche of the man / woman relationship but also reflects the importance of family life, with its meaningfulness, innocence and love. The Afsana "Darakhtu Wali Gali" amply covers this important aspect of life. While reading the Afsana, this sentence caught my eye and I could not resist reading it repeatedly: "*Beta aurat thak jaati hai, Maa nahi thakti.*" [Look, Son! A woman gets tired, but a mother doesn't.]

Dear Rabia! I have related your Afsanas to real life and identified the sensitive subjects that you focused to convey the naked realities of it. In the context of my own observations and experiences, I am a witness to the truth of your stories. I have a gut feeling that a dialogue and ultimately a friendship is possible between us. With this hope, I am sending you this first epistle. If this letter inspires you, it can be the starting point of our discourse. How do you like the idea?

An admirer of your Afsanas,

Khalid Sohail

Second Dream

A Pleasant Surprise

1ˢᵗ May 2018

Your letter was a pleasant surprise. Although I feel that the row of surprises has already culminated at nowhere than myself.

In today's fast-moving life, taking a few minutes to go through someone else's work is in fact devoting your precious time to the writer. It certainly is a great gesture. In my university days, I had read Khalid Sohail's articles while sitting on the library floor. Your name was fixed in my memory. I had never thought that two literary wanderers would ever come across each other on the Hum-Sub internet platform like this. On the contrary, life has taught me that nothing is impossible in this world. It would feel good to me if two creative minds could continue with the literary dialogue. Yet Time plays a vital role in our lives. At times one feels too feeble to deviate from the dictates of Time.

You have raised some questions in your letter. I will answer those soon. For now, suffice it to say that I find myself a quiet observer of life around me. I have been watching life dancing around and moving ahead, from the observatory of my self-imposed prison. It has continued for decades. The art of putting my observations into words is a blessing of my Creator. He, in his magnanimity, might have bestowed upon Rabia the talent of writing as a reward for her loneliness and solitude.

It seems to me as if the characters show up, tell me their tales and walk away. This might be the reason that I do not attach any meaning to eternity. I have a different understanding of life altogether. Certain lives do not measure up to the criteria of society. When they don't, the very criteria become questions for those people. I was entangled in such questions at a very young age. I was weak in oral expression and there was much I held inside. Then I found a weep hole through my pen. I started to deliver it on paper.

However, I was born with abundant love. The fragrance of love touched me like first touch of lovers, droplets of first summer-rain and fragrance of early spring flowers. I was the only daughter to receive all the love from my family. Some people are born to be loved yet the abundance of love has its own fetters. These shackles prevent you from living a life of your own choosing. I am perhaps one of those people... There is a hidden and strange feeling of sadness. While commenting on one of my *Afsanas* you talked about metaphors like Sin and Reward. I would like to add here that the meanings of Sin and Reward are quite different to a radical like me. To me, life itself looks like a sin at one time and a reward at another.

There was a time when Rabia was fond of Khalid Sohail's ideas as they were ripe with peace and tranquility. But after having spoken to you, I found that you have a keen interest in human psychology. It adds to my conviction that you are devoted to humanity and sincere to your profession.

You said you have the opportunities to meet various people and observe life closely. Rabia's life too has been taking her on a similar voyage of observation. Life is still treating her in the same manner. But Rabia's quest is quite different.

So far, I have concluded that there are certain waves that move humans along. These waves always reveal the truth. What we feel is always true. What we profess might not be. Any utterance not supported by an inner feeling is not true as it lacks sincerity. And any seed sown without sincerity can never make a strong tree.

Sincerely,

Rabia.

Third Dream

Rabia — A Character of Islamic Mythology

3rd May 2018

Rabia presents her Salam to Dervish!

Rabia is not just a name. Rather, it is a renowned character of Islamic mythology. This character is woven with the threads of an unknown obsession, a rigorous trail, an unbelievable belief and a symbol of altruistic love.

It's after midnight here. At this hour of the night two kinds of people usually remain wake a saint or a sinner. Who is who, should be decided on the Day of Judgment. Over here, cold winds are blowing with a tumultuous energy. The natural hide-and-seek of lightening and the thundering sound of clouds in the sky is urging a creative mind to scribble something on the waiting pad of paper. But the hard rigors of a day's work have tired me so badly that I cannot find enough wits to place a few petals of creativity on the paper.

My heart aches. I wish to cry but cannot... Such helplessness is at times unbearable. My heart is filled with pain. There is nothing else left in it than pain. The heart that pulsates in the chest of a sensitive writer feels the agony of others as well.

I have a question for Dervish. Like Prophets and Saints, are writers also born as writers? Or can someone become a writer through sheer hard work? If it could be done through struggle, then why can I not write whenever I wish to? Sometimes I hold a pen and paper for hours but cannot write a word, but on other occasions numerous pages are inked within a few minutes.

I am exhausted at this moment, but nature always overwhelms Rabia with all its facets. That is the reason my heart is telling me to write. My tiredness sitting across the far-away mountains, has whispered to my heart: "Creativity is your lifeline. You must write or else you will die." Hence, I wrote a letter to Dervish. Dervish who while sitting at the shrine of humanity, prays for rain, the rain that showers all without discrimination. It holds the message of the existence of an invisible Power.

Rabia will not wait for a reply from Dervish. The notion of waiting has long since faded from my life. The wait creates hope, and the hope brings an agony. I have no place left in my heart to endure any more pains.

I wonder how the weather is across the seas in Dervish's land. I do not even know whether it's day or night there. Over here it is just before dawn. There is a peace and quietness all over. An overwhelming force has arrived to take Rabia into its soothing arms for a slumber. Since Rabia needs to go with it, she says to Dervish, *Fi-Amaan-Allah* [Be in God's custody]. While doing so she is not even sure whether Dervish's and Rabia's God is the same or otherwise. But she leaves Dervish in her God's custody. To live one needs the eternal support of a Divine Power. Rabia is yet unaware of any greater Power than Allah. Her world is not very vast.

Rabia Al-Raba

Fourth Dream

Dervish – A Seeker of Truth

4th May 2018

Dervish presents his compliments to Rabia.

Dervish is a seeker of truth. As well, he is the holder of an idea, a wish, a message and a dream. Dervish embraces the idea of a peaceful and tranquil world. To achieve that, he seeks to promote love among humanity across the globe. Dervish also holds a dream of humanity evolving towards a harmonious world.

It was evening here when Dervish received Rabia's letter. Rabia lives in the East whereas Dervish dwells in the West. In Rabia's land when the sun is rising in the morning, the same is setting in Dervish's country. In this way, Rabia's letter travels backwards in the ocean of Time. When it is night for Rabia, Dervish is busy with his day's errands; yet both are connected regardless of clock time.

To Dervish, Rabia's name holds not only a magnetic attraction but a great mystery. Rabia is not just the name of a woman, it is a title assigned to an extra ordinary personality as well as a tradition. Dervish was introduced to Mystic Rabia Basri by his Sufi Father when he was just twelve. His father handed him *Tazkra tul Aulia* – 'The Stories of Saints' to read. The book mesmerized him, so much so, that he wrote the first essay of his life on Rabia Basri's personality and philosophy of life. He sent the article to a children's magazine of that time; "*Bachoo'n Ki Dunya*". Dervish's bliss reached its peak when the editor published his commentary on Rabia Basri. A similar happiness was felt when Dervish received Rabia's letter last evening. Dervish received Rabia's letter not only in the evening of the day but also in the evening of his life. He felt as if the cycle of Rabia's life has been completed. It is the cycle that is the symbol of infinity with neither a start nor an end. Dervish felt the aroma of two Rabias infused into each other.

Dervish recalled that in one of Rabia Basri's stories, there was a slave woman who served her earthly master all day long and worshiped her heavenly Lord the entire night. She was addicted to the nectar of love. When her earthly master learnt it, he freed her.

In another story, one day Rabia Basri was found running through the crowded city of Basra. She carried two pots, one containing fire and the other water. On someone's inquiry she replied; "I am going to burn Heaven to ashes with fire and quench Hell with water. People will no longer worship God due to fear of Hell or lust for Heaven. Rather, they should adore their Creator out of His sheer Love".

Dervish remembers another incident in the same book. Rabia Basri used to visit a Dervish who would urge his disciples: "Do not lose heart. Keep knocking, the door will open one day. Watching this for a while, one day Rabia addressed the Dervish: "O Dervish! Why do you tell your pupils to keep knocking? Did you not know that the door was never closed?"

Rabia Basri had acquired a very high spiritual status in the realm of *Tareeqat* [a tradition of mysticism that follows practices of earlier saints] and *Maarfat* [knowledge of religion and spirituality], a place extremely difficult if not impossible for ordinary men and women to acquire.

Dervish commenced his journey of creativity from the alley of mysticism. He then took the trail of literature that led him to the track of philosophy and ultimately the highway of psychology. On this highway another milestone awaited Dervish. He was astonished to learn that the word "psyche" that meant' "soul" in ancient religions is now understood as "mind" in the contemporary world.

Rabia has quizzed Dervish: "Like the prophets and saints, are writers also born as writers? Or can someone become a writer through sheer hard work?" I felt as if Rabia believes in a divine Father who sends his Messengers to guide his children on earth. And Dervish opines that humans are not children of a divine Father, rather they are wards of the Mother Earth.

Dervish is of the view that every child has some creative capability. Some children have this capability more than others. The creative talent is like a seed. It goes without saying that every seed needs the requisite light, water, air and rigorous care to become a strong tree. Similarly, every child needs loving parents, kind teachers, free land and a peaceful society to actualize his potential to become a poet, scientist or scholar. But if you clip the wings of a baby hawk, at best it would become a pigeon.

Dervish surmises that creativity, insanity and spirituality are mystically and mysteriously connected. In this realm of connection, the insane and the creator of a scripture sit on the same pedestal. Poetry becomes an important attribute of prophet-hood.

From numerous intellectual discourses with his poet uncle Arif Abdul Mateen and through his own reading, experiences and observations, Dervish has arrived at the conclusion that there are three ways to reach the ultimate wisdom or the truth. These are namely: Intuition, used by ascetics and mystics; Aesthetic, used by poets and artists; and Logic used, by the scientists. A scientist first feels the truth, then he expresses it in words, and finally proceeds to prove it through research. In this manner a scientist in fact strives to model an intuitive reality into an objective reality. He knows that to believe in an intuitive truth, one needs faith more than logic. On the contrary, countless simple souls have blind faith in centuries-old dogmas and waste their lives in aimless wandering. A sincere mystic, a real scientist and a virtuous poet respect each other's truth.

At the dawn of his life Dervish believed that there is only one truth, and that truth is the last and eternal reality. But at the dusk of his life he has concluded that there are as many truths in this world as there are people. Hence Dervish is trying to figure out Rabia's truth which is based on her sincerity and experiences. Like Rabia Basri, all night she remains immersed in thoughts, creative exertion and worship. Dervish has been reading biographies of scientists, scholars, poets, thinkers and mystics. He has arrived at the crux of how much toil, sweat and exertion is needed to reach the zenith of one's art. He likes Albert Einstein's saying: "Creativity is 1% inspiration and 99% perspiration."

Dervish knows many such artists who have sacrificed precious years and decades of their lives rigorously working to acquire mastery over their craft. Dervish considers it their homework to become a successful poet or a scholar. Dervish knows that the expression of his art is a matter of life and death for an artist. Rabia's letter reminds him of Abbas Tabish's couplet:

Skoot e Dahr raggo'n mein utter gya hota

Agar mein Sheyr na kehta tou mar gya hota

The poisonous solitude of the world had run into my veins

Not reciting my poetry would have turned me into remains

Throughout his life Dervish has been striving to know the secrets of life, death, love, hatred, friendship, enmity and poetry. He is smelling a fragrance of friendship from Rabia's letter. Dervish is recalling his grandmother's saying: "One and one do not make two, rather, they make eleven."

Dervish asked Rabia about the beginning of her intellectual journey. How had she embarked upon the flight of creativity? How has travelling on the path of creativity affect her personal life? What sacrifices has she had to render to become a writer? But sleep is inviting Dervish and he doesn't want to annoy her. He therefore wishes to take his leave of Rabia until the next letter.

Goodnight.

Fifth Dream

The One Who Reads People, Becomes a Dervish

10th May 2018

Rabia says Salam to Dervish!

Rabia envies Dervish who lives a free life; she is enslaved by an earthly master. Although her heavenly Creator has given her insight into an infinite intuitive freedom, these few moments are limited to solitary nights. Perhaps her earthly master has not yet witnessed Rabia conversing with her heavenly Lord, so she has yet to be granted freedom.

O Dervish! Its 3 AM with me. It's the time when stars shine more intensely. They appear glowing and twinkling. Then an incandescent star appears on the horizon to announce that it's the time for mating, the infusing of two times into each other. Then the two times, night and day, move into each other's cozy embrace. The red color is splashed all over the horizon to celebrate the union, like the face of a shy bride during her lovemaking with her lover. Then they part ways. The redness turns white as the day brightens up. The hot emotions subside to a satisfying coolness.

O Dervish! You have answered my question in the most elaborate manner. It has entirely satisfied me to the depths of my aesthetic sensibilities. You have also asked a few questions. For my response, I could write a small book. But Rabia, an intellectually free captive, has no time for herself to write even a booklet. She wishes to reply in leaflets. If she desires to answer your questions in a few words, it would be something like this...

Rabia had never thought of becoming a writer. Rather, she wished to become a painter. The colors haunted her, be they of art, life or nature. But she owned none of these. This lack was in a way a sacrifice of her life as well as her feminine nature. It was a sacrifice of her dreams and her emotions.

Rabia tried her best to live a normal life, the life of an ordinary girl. She wished to walk on the highway of life bare-footed. But it never happened. Now she feels that she was and still is in the grip of an unknown force — a power that raises walls in the path of her longings and desires. She cannot surmount those barriers. For her entire life Rabia was denied what she wished for, be it love, happiness or any other desire. But in turn, Nature has been bestowing upon her what she had never thought of. As they say: "When God takes away something precious from you, He rewards you in an unimaginable manner." This is the law of nature.

Then a time arrived when Rabia understood Rabia Basri's saying: "Without God's, will one cannot regret his or her sins." She also understood the stories of the ancient Prophets Yousef and Moses. Prophet Yousef had a dream that he was thrown into a ditch by his siblings where he could have been a feast for desert wolves. Instead he came out alive, purchased by the merchants of a caravan and sold to Aziz, the King of Egypt. He lived rest of his life in the palace of a king, in the most protected environment. It was made possible by the invisible Power that holds the strings of "possible" and "impossible." Rabia also understood the tale of Moses. His mother put the infant Moses in a wooden box and left it to float along the waters of the River Nile. How was it possible that he reached the palace of Pharaoh? He too was raised in the palace by the King who was supposed to kill him in his very infancy. Therefore, Rabia unknowingly lived all her life hanging between possibilities and impossibilities.

O Dervish! A few days back Rabia was discussing *Tassawaf* [mysticism] with Irfan Ul Haq Sahib. From nowhere the word Dervish came under discussion. Irfan

Sahib explained: "The one who reads books becomes learned and the one who reads people becomes a Dervish." So you have embarked upon a journey of reading people.

In his previous letter Dervish wrote about Rabia Basri. Yes, this Rabia too has a passionate love for the Saint. She adores her, rather idealizes her to the extent that she had pledged in her youth that if Rabia ever had a daughter she would name her after Rabia Basri.

This Rabia (I) was the first daughter on both sides of her family. Her uncle wished to name the girl after a woman the like of whom did not exist in history. He named his only niece after Rabia Basri –Rabia. As Rabia grew up, her love for the mystical Saint intensified. It was a passionate attachment with the historical mystic woman. This Rabia searched for Rabia Basri's books. She found some poetry of Basri and translated it into Urdu.

Rabia was delighted and impressed when she read about Rabia Basri's prime times. In one of the myths, Allah ordered the Kaaba to receive Rabia Basri on the eve of her pilgrimage. One is in awe of the spiritual pedestal occupied by the greatest mystic woman of her time. Men everywhere wish to dominate women. They inflict atrocities on their women. Such a need to control women is driven by the fear of great women like Rabia Basri in the history of mankind.

O Dervish! Rabia has understood the power of a woman by *Khulah* [right of a wife to demand a divorce from her husband]. On such a demand she is not questioned. The gifts are returned, and becomes free. On the contrary, in case of divorce by the husband, it's a hectic process. Despite his resentment, many a time he remains living in a hateful union. Hence nature protects the will of the woman. The creator has made a strange psyche. If love leaves a woman's heart the ocean of love turns into the barren rocks. Every sound turns back like an echo. The fertile land changes into barren soil.

The man keeps sowing the seeds of his bad behavior towards his partner. The weeds of hatred secretly grow in the soil of their relationship. Then a day comes when it becomes impossible to enjoy a loving relationship. In my land the respect for a woman has never been accepted. It remains a dream. Over here she is neither Eve, Ayesha, Khadija, Maryam, Asya nor Rabia. She is a just a physical body. The body has learnt to deceive her counterpart. It has got away from its natural and soulful manifestation. Therefore, both men and women here are miserably looking for true love in each other.

O Dervish! Alas, we view a person beyond what lies between our thighs to make this world lust-free and peaceful.

O Dervish! An English story writer and fiction translator, Colonel Naeem Ashraf, is a literary friend of mine. The other day we talked about a picture that showed the Fairmont Springs Hotel in Banff, a tourist resort two hours' drive from Calgary. History reveals that hundred years ago a railway was laid in that mountainous part of Canada. The laborers worked in minus temperatures with no decent shelter. As they say, "Necessity is the mother of invention." Canadians built this eight-story building in stone. Eye witnesses note that even after a hundred years, the structure has not deviated an inch from its origin.

Yet the modern world, O Dervish is progressing at god speed, leaving behind the stone buildings. Science is endeavoring to reach the planets beyond the Moon. Having fulfilled his dream of flying in the air like a bird, man is now busy exploring the depths of the seas and all of planet Earth. I am a firm believer that the day is not far off when the science will prove the very existence of God in physical shape. That would be Doomsday. But shall the dwellers of Rabia's land ever evolve intellectually? Or would we remain engrossed talking about the success stories of developed nations? Will humanity ever smile in my land or would Rabia acquire salvation, being a believer by birth?

Over here, dawn is about to break. The "incandescent star" is drifting away to some unknown space. Soon the reddish horizon caused by the mating of two moments will change into a silky white. Then the above 40-degree temperature will start burning bodies and souls. Humans are happy having deforested the countryside to build wide highways, roads and plazas. It has caused global warming to the degree of hell-fire heat. They call it progress.

Rabia takes leave of Dervish as she fears light and gets perturbed. She cannot face light.

O Dervish! Allah be with you.

Sixth Dream

Four Dreams

11th May 2018

Dervish presents his compliments to Rabia.

Rabia's letter kept Dervish in a mist of gloom for quite a while. Dervish recalled the early days of his life. Those days were dark and gloomy. Then a ray of hope shone into his heart from somewhere. It brightened up every cell of his body. In those days, Dervish lived with his parents Ayesha and Basit along with his younger sister Amber in Peshawar - a traditional city of Pakistan. His family resided on a river bank. Going for long walks and reflecting on life was the favorite hobby of Dervish. One evening, walking on the bank of the river, Dervish suddenly realized that life was a precious gift that it should not be wasted. He wished to live a purposeful life. Dervish resolved to dream about his wish list. Then he saw four dreams.

Dervish's first dream was to become a psychiatrist, a Messiah who could acquire insights to resolve the intricate knots between the human body, mind and subconscious, in order to help reduce suffering in people's lives by restoring their physical and mental health. Dervish's second dream was to become a poet and scholar who would be able to read the works of writers, poets and philosophers across the globe. Dervish wished to write not one book but many. He dreamt of many people looking for his books just as he visits libraries to look for his favorite writers. Then he would be adding a few drops into the ocean of knowledge and literature.

Dervish's third dream was to take a world tour to meet people of various races and cultures. He wished to become a well-travelled and experienced man who knew "the ways of the world".

Dervish's fourth dream was to befriend men, women, writers, poets and artists from all over the world. He wished to write down the stories of their passions, pleasures and agonies. Dervish had envisaged these dreams in the morning of his life. Now that he is entering the evening of his life, he looks back and recalls Faiz Ahmed Faiz's couplet:

Faiz thi rah sar basar Manzil

Ham Jehan pohnchay kamyab aaey

O Faiz! The goal anxiously awaited us on the way

Wherever we ventured, success met us on the way

Dervish considers himself a fortunate person who in his youth saw his childhood dreams turning into reality. Now, he is come true a dream of many years which he had called "Literary Love Letters". The dream was of writing a book containing his and Rabia's creative letters. In his mind Rabia's character was fictitious. He had never thought that he would find a real Rabia, also a writer, who would join him to turn his creative dream into reality. Dervish is thankful to Rabia from the bottom of his heart for joining him, as he could not have accomplished this dream all by himself. Being a writer, Dervish has known for a long time that "Letter Fiction" as a genre of literature could not find a place compared to poetry, the short story and the novel, possibly because it requires two people, preferably from opposite genders, to accomplish this kind of creative work.

Dervish now thinks, it was relatively easy for him as a male to migrate from the East to the West. For the sake of their dreams and wishes every artist has to sacrifice something. But if the cost of dreams and wishes is an Eastern woman, the price is more adorable. In this context

Dervish recognizes Rabia's struggle and expresses his gratitude to her. Dervish had written the story of his migration from the East to the West in the preface of his second collection of poetry, *Azad Fizaein* [free atmosphere] in following words:

"To test the force of my flight

I asked my surroundings, freedom and height"

The courage to fly: On awakening from a carefree slumber, a bird found that he sat in a nest made from the straws of outmoded customs and weeds of decayed values. It looked like an abode but in fact it was a prison. He passed his days and nights on a tree grown by ghosts of the family taboos. The tree itself was part of an orchard cum prison. As in a dark cave, the buds could not blossom, the morning breeze never blew, and the moon was not seen rising. Spring was never seen smiling. The entire place was engulfed by the suffocation, darkness and ambience of autumn. As the bird gained more awareness it was revealed to him that he was not allowed to see with his eyes, listen with his ears or think with his mind. He was neither supposed to sing nor allowed to fly.

It was painful for the bird to know that earlier on, a few birds had attempted to fly from the nest but failed, as either their wings were clipped, or they had pierced by the hunters' arrows. He also came to realize that there were others who did not have the courage to fly away. They just died of banging their heads against the weeds of the nest. The bird was perplexed. He neither wanted to be game for hunters nor wished to bang his head and die. Rather, he desired to fly off to a place where he could breathe the fresh air, smell the fragrance of flowers, listen to the music of a flowing stream, witness the moonlight and enjoy the spring.

A few old birds told him that the birds who had earlier become victims of hunters did wish to break the shackles of their past but lacked a clear vision of the future. They were fed up with the darkness but did not have enough courage to embrace the light. To acquire the right altitude for the flight, it was imperative that they dive deeper into their souls but it was beyond their capacity. The bird took a long time to prepare himself for his upcoming flight. Then a day came when he took off from his nest with full force. Soon, he had left his native town far behind in a single flight. When he passed over mountains, valleys, rivers and jungles, the bird viewed many cities beneath him. In every city he found two kinds of people: wailing people those of his hometown and rejoicing people who sang the songs of freedom.

The bird is happy that in his flight to higher destinations, other birds are also joining him. Slowly the single flight would become a flock. It is his earnest desire to raise his altitude and while doing so, encourage those birds who prepare for it.

Right now, Dervish is sitting in his clinic. This is the room where he meets his "muse" who brings him literary gifts every day. Dervish calls this place a creative labor room. Rabia probably does not know that before becoming a psychiatrist in Canada, Dervish worked in the labor room of a female hospital in Peshawar. During the job, Dervish became familiar with the labor-pains. In those days he wrote many poems about the women. To let Rabia know Dervish's connection with women's creative and humanistic aspect, Dervish wishes to share a poem with her:

The Tears of Blood

Women fight the battle of survival all the time
They are perpetually playing a blood-game all the time
Every month, when the calamity surpasses them
They find lava flowing inside them

Life sends women every month an epistle

They find their fate inscribed in that epistle

They are told they should know their true worth

Bear children, become mothers to, have some worth

If women refuse they are told to choose

Either they stay barren or shed tears of blood

They always rest in the ambience of tears

Women are pictures, stories of pain

Women are scriptures written with pain

In response to Rabia's letter, Dervish wishes to write more, but he must see his patients. It's time to get back to his job. Dervish requests leave from Rabia, awaiting her next letter. Dervish is curious to know what kind of creative dream Rabia has had, of and how she felt having learnt about Dervish's dream.

Seventh Dream

The Dream Realizer

13th May 2018

Rabia presents her greetings to Dervish!

Its midnight here, like any other summer night, short and crisp. Rabia has no idea when she first started to wish she lived somewhere where the night would last at least twelve hours. As the night darkens, Rabia feels a growing freedom in its lap. But as it moves towards the next day, Rabia feels herself quivering in the invisible vice of her captivity. Over here the summers are long, with short nights. No sooner do you start feeling night's ambience, it has already left without saying goodbye, like an unfaithful lover.

On Dervish's reference to a river, Rabia recalls her childhood days. When she was a toddler, her family resided near the famous Lahore Canal that passes through the middle of the city. After supper, her Baba would take her for a stroll on the Canal Bank Road. He would narrate to her the stories of old Lahore, of its history and architecture. Rabia once wrote about those good old times in one of her literary columns:

"My Baba was the first person to introduce me to Lahore. He told me that the Mall Road (now) was called Cool Road in past days. Tangas (horse carriages) used to elegantly ply this road. The Canal Bank Road used to breathe in dewed nights and provide a haven for passers-by in the summer afternoons. Holding the finger of my baba, I walked along the Canal for hours. In those times the roads were not infested with maddened traffic calling for their widening through cutting lush green trees. The green belt too was quite wider in those days. The road leading to India had little traffic plying its narrow chest even after crossing the famous Ferozepur Road. We used to walk up to

Shah Jamal. Baba used to tell me the history of FC College, Jamia Ashrafia and PCSIR Building that we saw on our way. It all seems dancing in my memory lanes. The Canal is still flowing on the same course. But it has now been confined by concrete shoulders. Like its past, it doesn't flow freely singing and emitting music with the falling rain droplets. Now, the natural façade has been altered by artificiality. The old ambience stayed till few decades back. Until recently, The Mall Road and Bank Canal Road both had an air of romance due to the tall trees on their shoulder, which seemed whispering to nature. Lahorites called it the River Tames and Punjabi poets attached Punjabi songs to the romance of the Canal, such as:

Sanu nehar walay pull tay bula kay

Te khawarray maai kithay reh gya...

Over the Canal Bridge we had to meet

But I can't find my lover for the treat!

Despite the maddened traffic all the time on the Canal Bank Road, the morning walkers still find solace in the sight of the Canal in the dim light of the early hours. When the Sun shines its first rays on the Canal's clayed water, you find paper boats floating in the middle, carrying fresh flower petals. Someone sitting on the brink upstream might be setting those flower-filled paper boats on the flowing water. With the sunshine falling on them, the floating flowers present an awesome scene on the surface of the water.

Few land into the right hands; the others wait near the bank to be picked up by a wandering lover, and there are few of them who not finding an admirer, choose to disappear under the water. A jungle silence prevailed once around the area where the Canal intersects the Muslim Town- Garden Town Road. There was quietness even during broad day light. But now the crowded roads have drowned out the serenity and romance. The roads tremble with the cacophony of grinding them down. The Canal Bank Road has been widened by removing lush green trees yet seems to be short of accommodating the ever-swelling population and its commuting needs.

The Daily Jinnah – 14 October 2015

In those times the Canal and the city of Lahore were not like as they are now. Now the so-called pace of progress has turned the humans, fora and fauna into materialistic beings. Today's generation likes to eat Chinese, American, Russian and Italian junk food but hate home-made-ghee, naturally grown vegetables and fresh fruits. This age of materialism has made life difficult. It seems easy to die. Rabia wishes to dwell at a place where she doesn't have to drink mineral water. The tap water should be as good as the mineral water.

Dervish wrote of his long-awaited dreams coming true. He also talked about his last dream, the dream of having creative letter writing with a female counterpart - Rabia. Rabia too had a similar dream. She had dreamt of exchanging creatively written letters with an intelligent and open-minded man. Rabia thought such discourse was only possible between man and a woman, as new life can only take birth through the union of male and female. But unfortunately, Rabia lives in society where open-minded men are hard to find. You only find males (This is her own speculation). They consider woman a female's body. The men in Rabia's world are so desperate for women that if it were possible they would take their favorite women with them into their graves.

Rabia belongs to a society where she had remained intellectually covered with the colorful attire of hypocrisy. She cannot have an intellectual discourse with men lest she become trapped, a victim of their lust. The woman of Rabia's society is very aware that she should not talk wisdom. Here intellectual discourses are seen as mental vulgarity and literary exchanges are considered lechery by women. The status of a vulgar woman in this world is very well known to Dervish as well as Rabia. The friendship of historical characters Hassan Basri and Rabia Basri always haunted Rabia. She wondered whether it was possible for an intellectual man and woman of today to have a spiritual connection and a literary friendship.

Rabia felt happy to read Dervish's dreams. She felt even happier to know that all Dervishes' dreams turned into reality. Dervish talked of his first flight. Rabia too had thought of such a flight but could not do that. She felt that at the verge of flight she was either turned into iron, water, a cloud or just the air. In that state she forgot to fly. Rabia surrendered to the circumstances. At last, like the mother of Prophet Moses, she handed herself to the river of fate. When Rabia talks of these facts of her life she is not presenting her grievances. Nature has bestowed upon her blessings without her needing to take flight. Such bounties are not available to many girls of her age. When Rabia ponders the blessings she intensely recalls the lives of Prophet Yousef and Rabia Basri.

Rabia has learnt through her experience that time tests the intensity of your love in one form or the other. If you succeed in the test, the sight of your love-path is crystal clear. Rabia has a firm belief that the attributes of your ideal person invisibly infuse into you. While requesting leave, Rabia quizzes Dervish whether her belief is true.

O Dervish! The early dawn star is about to appear. Rabia wishes to sleep. There might be a dream waiting for Rabia. It is possible that she dreams of something that might turn into reality like that of Dervish's dreams.

Fee Amaan Allah [Stay in God's safe hands]

Eighth Dream

Hello, Adaab, Salaam

14th May 2018

Dervish presents to Rabia a friendly Salam!

Since the start of his correspondence with Rabia, Dervish is perpetually pondering over the effectiveness and uniqueness of the "Words". Dervish always says: 'Hello' to Canadian friends, 'Adaab' to Indian friends, then he considers it no harm to say 'Salam' to Pakistani friends. Rabia always says Salaam to start a letter and ends with *Fi-Amaan-Illah*. This reminds Dervish of an interesting story. He once came across an older female patient. She was a Canadian and an expert in linguistics who enjoyed a command over the origin and history of English words. I asked her, "Why do we say Goodbye in English whereas we say, *Allah Hafiz e Shuma* in Persian, *Allah Hafiz* in Urdu and *Rab Raakha* in Punjabi? The old lady replied: "In the beginning "Goodbye" too was 'God be with you', it was however modified to due to excessive use and secular tradition".

Dervish has observed that his secular, atheist friends sometimes say *Khuda Hafiz* while parting. In this regard, I am reminded of a verse:

Samajh na lena kay mujh ko bohat aqeedat hai

Woh aaditan tha jo naam e Khuda lya meinay

Never think that I am a faithful

My reference to God was a ritual

Dervish is astonished to read Rabia's letters. At such a young age, how did Rabia's personality acquire such depth and wisdom? It is perhaps a reward for her meditation, reflecting upon the mysteries of life during secluded, lonely and sleepless nights, following the tradition of her ideal - Rabia Basri. She has acquired the mastery of staying awake at night. In return life has awarded her the insight to see through the darkness. This is a sign of wisdom. Dervish had once said: *"Wisdom is the inner light that helps people see in the dark."*

It gives Dervish immense pleasure to know that Rabia trusts him. Faith in other person is in fact a foundation stone of a true friendship. While reading Rabia's letters, Dervish often muses, that he meets numerous people in his life but knows only a few and feels intimacy with none. They stay strangers to Dervish. On the contrary, Dervish has never met Rabia, yet feels so intimate that he smells a fragrance of friendship as if he knows her for ages. Dervish wishes to ask Rabia: "What is the secret behind such intimacy?"

Dervish agrees with Rabia's idea that when you idealize a person, you unknowingly adopt certain attributes of your ideal. It reminds him of a professor of the University of Toronto who once told him, "When the students carry out research on poets, writers or scholars, they need to go through their biographies and works. While doing so, they unconsciously acquire the personality traits of these intellectuals. It is a strange phenomenon that they invisibly also adopt their philosophy and way of life."

Dervish is curious to know about the creative life of Rabia. When he reads her short stories, he feels that Rabia flies on the wings of her conscious and subconscious simultaneously. Dervish also longs to know when it was revealed to Rabia that an artist, and a writer dwell inside her. What was the reaction of her friends, relatives, writers and critics when Rabia embarked upon her literary journey?

When Dervish is free from his job, he sometimes visits Dervish's Inn where he meets other Dervishes. On other occasions Dervish organizes seminars to meet and greet poets, artists and scholars visiting from other cities and countries. Dervish surmises that the creative minority that follows the voice of the heart need constant support and cooperation from like-minded people. Otherwise under the social pressure of the traditional majority they might lose their wits like famous poet Mir Taqi Mir or commit suicide like Sylvia Plath, Earnest Hemingway and Vincent Van Gogh. Very few people are aware of the sacrifices and hardships of the creative minority. The realm of creativity is a double-bladed sword. In the words of Arif Abdul Mateen:

Meri azmat ka nishan , meri tabahi ki daleel

Mein ne halaat kay saanchu mein na dhala khud ko

The reasons of my glory or defeat might be the same

I never tried to fit into the environmental frame

Dervish is looking out of his window. Wonderful weather is inviting him to have a long stroll. During his long walks, fresh thoughts quietly make their way into Dervish's mind.

Therefore, Dervish requests a break from Rabia.

Ninth Dream

Fragrance of Friendship

15th May 2018

Rabia says Salam to Dervish!

Rabia seeks pardon for a late reply. She was trapped in useless and futile obligations that have no bearing on life nor death...

Question about wisdom first brought a smile to Rabia's face. Then she recalled an anecdote attributed to Socrates. Its authenticity is uncertain, yet she found it interesting. Someone asked Socrates the secret behind his wisdom. Socrates suggested the man visit his home. So one day, the man went to Socrates's place, no sooner had he reached the door, he heard a female yelling abusive and foul language. Appalled, the man left. On another day, as Socrates was lecturing his students, the man walked up to him and told him about his visit and hearing the yelling. The great philosopher said: "She is my wife and that is the secret of my wisdom". Similarly, if there is an iota of wisdom about Rabia, the secret might be her dwelling in her surroundings.

Rabia wishes to tell Dervish that she believes in the myth of "Spirits' Tribes". She must have already met Dervish in the world of spirits. Rabia also believes that their spirits come from same tribe. That's why there is no estrangement and a sweet fragrance of friendship is felt by both. All over the universe, the creative people belong to the same tribe. Moreover, Rabia has a gut feeling that she was a wandering soul in the realm of souls. That could be yet another reason for not feeling unfamiliar while meeting new people on Earth.

Like Dervish, Rabia always wanted to travel, not only on Earth but into the skies. So far it has not been possible physically, but she always travelled intellectually. She is subconsciously on a flight to unknown destinations while looking at trees, doing household errands, sipping her tea or coffee. Rabia is on a journey of the soul since her early childhood. When she was a small child she used to catch glowworms from the plants grown in her garden and watch them at length. On moonlit nights, Rabia used to go up on the roof top or sit on the stairs and count the galaxies of stars across the sky. She sometimes watched three in-line stars on the eastern horizon and wondered where the Sun could have reached by that time and would there be clouds also wandering in a certain part of sky. Such was her journey of thought and intimacy with the Nature at that age.

Rabia was a sole sister with no similar age male or female child to play with. She was alone but never felt lonely, although she grew up as a quiet child. She felt a whole world revolving around her seclusion. She did not like any interference in her small world. Rabia was annoyed with even a small intervention into her seclusion. Rabia could overcome this only habit with the passage of time.

Then Rabia recalls the story of her intimacy with her father. She was only eight when her father had to go abroad. Rabia fell sick. She suffered from chest pain. The doctor's efforts were bearing no fruit until a chest specialist asked her mother about her father. When he was told that Rabia's father was out of the country, the doctor advised her mother to urge Rabia to start writing letters to her father. Rabia complied with the doctor's prescription and it worked. Her innocent letters were collected and posted by her mother to her father. She slowly started to recover, and her chest pain completely subsided. She kept writing even after her father arrived home. But the writing now turned into diary writing. To start with she wrote about her daily happenings, then she shifted to dream-writing. She used to keep her diary hidden, maybe because of her young age. Then on one fine morning Rabia started to paint. She perhaps acquired this habit from her father who himself was a painter. She won all the painting contests in her school and college days. She wished to become a painter. She wanted to join the National College of Arts, but she was denied the opportunity.

Badly hurt, Rabia decided to quit education; but things have their own dynamics. As fate would have it, her painting talent continued its manifestation in the form of calligraphy. She taught calligraphy to Montessori classes besides continuing her education. Then Rabia entered the Government College Lahore (also called Asian Oxford) as student of Urdu literature. . By that time, she had become an amateur writer. She wrote light poetry and sent her essays for the literary pages of various Newspapers but had yet not authored a book. She was inducted into literary society of GC and ended up co-author of The Ravi, a literary college magazine. It enhanced her literary passion. When it came to her final year thesis, Asghar Nadeem Syed was appointed her supervisor. Rabia wished to write her thesis on male characters. To this end she went to Sohail Ahmed Khan for guidance. Sohail Ahmed advised her "If you wish to write on the male psyche you need to first create those characters." But till then she had only read a secondary class of male characters. However, she succeeded in writing on Ahmed Qasmi's few characters. By then Ahmed Nadeem Qasmi had passed away but his famous magazine *Funoon* was still publishing.

Since Rabia had to write her thesis, she met all the writers associated with Funoon. Qasmi Sahib's close associate Mansura Ahmed became a close friend. She encouraged Rabia to write as she had the potential. Then Amjad Islam Amjad, who had read her amateur poetry also encouraged Rabia to write prose. The work on her thesis was still in progress when Mansura Ahmed asked Rabia to send a story for the magazine every week. Rabia wrote a somewhat comic story based on an eye witness account which was accepted with little change. One day, Mansura advised Rabia: "Gurya! (Rabia's nickname in her college days) Get married. This world is too cruel for delicate people like you." At that moment, Rabia just laughed off the idea, but in later years she admitted the value of experienced advice. But again, marriage is an accident. At times it suddenly occurs, while for others it does not happen at all.

Rabia successfully did her Masters from Asian Oxford. She now dreamed of joining actual Oxford. Once again, her dreams were buried like a living *Anarkali. It reminds Rabia of her College's annual musical program. She appeared on stage wearing skin color spiraled pajama, red shirt and a dupatta. After the function, the students named her *Anarkali* of the GC (Government College Lahore). Rabia had not imagined that she, like *Anarkali* would be buried behind the bricks of the wall built by family taboos. Rabia's kind teacher Asghar Nadeem Syed wished to see her a lecturer in GC. But by then the "wall" had been built far above the head of *Anarkali*. At Syed's suggestion Rabia cried. Syed forcefully impressed upon her, "You have only one way left, write, write and write till your words start to speak."

Now Rabia feels the force of that moment which came to be a benediction. Baba also wanted her to become a writer. He used to narrate to Rabia the great stories of the female writers of his time. When she was only thirteen, Rabia occasionally stole the books from his library to read in a hideout. As luck would have it, the first book that she could lay her hand on was Khalil Jibran's. Rabia did not understand what she read, yet enjoyed it. Then she read Yousef Zuleika. She fell in love with Yousef to the point that she used to see him in her dreams, with the stars and the moon. It was like a teenager's one-sided love.

In the mythological love story of Yousef Zuleika, Yousef was considered a coward by a people of certain mindset. Notwithstanding, Rabia considers him the bravest man. The same mindset calls Zuleika a crazy woman due to her lustful advances towards Yousef. But Rabia views Zuleika as helpless and mesmerized by the handsome Yousef. Rabia opines that these two historical characters did not depict common man-woman psychology. They were different. Their psyches were different. Another letter is needed to write the complete account of Rabia's love for Yousef.

The rainy wet night is about to pass here. As the stars prepare to welcome the next day the clouds, after shedding tears all night, have gone to sleep. Before the sky gets whiter like the blood of selfish people, Rabia is hurrying to have a word with her Creator, therefore requests to take a leave of Dervish.

Fi Ammaan Allah

---

* Anarkali was a beautiful singer / dancer who performed in the court of Mughal Emperor Akbar. Prince Jahangir fell in love with Anarkali and wished to marry her. The King opposed it, and as the story goes, buried her alive in the brick line of the Fort.

Tenth Dream

Daughter of Heavenly Father and Son of Mother Earth

15th May 2018

Dervish presents Adaab to Rabia!

Having read Rabia's reference to 'the world of spirits', Dervish imagined that Rabia was the daughter of a Heavenly Father and Dervish the son of Mother Earth. Dervish also surmised that Rabia's relatedness to her heavenly father is as intimate, complicated and cumbersome as with her earthly father. That might have been the reason for her suffering from "separation anxiety" when her earthly father went abroad when she was just a kid. The advice of an earthly Messiah to write letters to her earthly father was a blessing in disguise. These letters not only eased Rabia's psychological ailment but also drove her toward writing. Rabia's letters first took the shape of a diary but ended up as short stories. Rabia's stories amply introduced the creative personality of Rabia to Dervish.

Dervish was really hurt to learn that Rabia was denied the opportunities to realize her dreams. About this situation, he recalled his own couplet:

Is darja rawayat ki dewarein uthaeen

Naslu se kisi shax ne bahir nhi dekha

Walls of traditions were built so tall and strong

For generations no one has seen out and beyond

It was Rabia's sheer luck that she was mentored by great writers like Asghar Nadeem Syed, Amjad Islam Amjad, Mansura Ahmed and Ahmed Nadeem Qasmi. They not only encouraged her but also polished her talent as a writer. While reading Rabia's letter Dervish also recalled his student days at Khyber Medical College –

Peshawar where he had taken part in the first poetry recital of his life. The jury consisted of Ahmed Nadeem Qasmi, Ahmed Faraz and Mohsin Ehsan. When Dervish was called upon to read his poem the audience was silent. The hall remained quiet during the recital of his poem. At the end however, there was an outburst of applause as Dervish was awarded the first prize - a statue of Venus. The name of Dervish's first poem was "Red Circle". Dervish wishes to reproduce his first poem here:

Today it was the seventeenth

The day brought worrisome thoughts for me

All day long

The pangs of suspicion kept creeping into my head

I was stunned and worried

Should I believe it or not?

I was perplexed since morning

This went on throughout the day

I wandered in my home, lost in my apprehensions

With deluded thoughts and fears

Then in the afternoon I went to my room

To turn over the calendar page with a trembling hand

I saw the thirteenth of the last month with a red circle

But this time my whole body quivered

With unknown fears

Then I cooled myself with a thought

It was only the seventeenth today

After writing the poem, Dervish realized that it was the tale of a woman. He then realized that there was perhaps a woman dwelling inside him. That might be the reason for his befriending more women than men. Most friends call him *Saheeli* [female friend] instead of Sohail. Rabia's letter also reminded Dervish of his meeting with Asghar Nadeem Syed at Sang E Meel Publishers when Syed invited him to deliver a lecture to the students of psychology in GC. When Dervish went to lecture the students, he was surprised to learn that there were more girls than boys.

Dervish still remembers his days in Lahore when he had many memorable meetings with Asghar Nadeem Syed, Kishwar Nahid, Munir Niazi and Zahid Dar.

Rabia thinks that marriage is an accident. Well, Dervish would like to ask her about love and marriage. Did she ever fall in love with someone or vice versa? What does she think of becoming a wife or a mother? Dervish has never dreamt of becoming a father or starting a family for that matter. He has always taken creative and literary friends as his family. Dervish calls it "Family of the Heart". One such friend is added to the family each year. This time, he is so happy to have with him the friend of the year that is Rabia.

Dervish must prepare for a seminar, therefore requests a leave from Rabia.

Eleventh Dream

Love and Dreams Never Exhaust You

18th May 2018

It is the holy month of Ramadan here. This is a busy month for Muslims as they perform religious rituals more vigorously than in other months. The practice of fasting is found in almost all religions in one form or another. It should have taught patience, restraint and content, but it has not worked. People around the globe seem busy as bees, piling up wealth, edibles and resources. They take pride in consuming their energies in lustful pursuits.

Dervish had asked a "unique question" in his last letter. Well Rabia cannot answer his question right away as she does not find herself focused now. Her world is divided into many segments. She does not find any space for herself. It was Friday yesterday. After a monotonous night, Rabia went to sleep at about the crack of dawn. Her slumber took her on a journey of beautiful destinations. So, when Rabia awoke she felt refreshed. The feeling of lovingness and the dreams never let her tire. Had there been no dreams, the life would have been so hard.

In the last part of her dream Rabia was reminded of a painful episode that occurred during last Ramadan, when a literary oppressor had tried to catch her in an evil scheme. Fortunately the fellow himself fell into the ditch dug for Rabia — the devastation and defeat is built into in any evil design. If people understood this, nobody would think badly of others. Someone asked Rabia Basri: "Have you ever seen who you worship?" She replied: "Why would I worship, if I do not see him?" At times the eyes cannot see what is witnessed by visionaries. Life is a beautiful gift of nature and solace is so precious. It cannot be bought with money.

Dervish says he had never wished to become a father or start a family. Rabia asks: "When did that first time occur to him? What is the climax of love between a man and a woman? Does the phenomenon of love exist in reality?" From her observations, Rabia has concluded that to a man, love is nothing more than bodily pleasure. He cannot even differentiate between lust and romance. Every man needs a sex partner in the garb of love. To Rabia love is a complete package that holds all seasons of gloom and pleasures alike. Bearing such apprehensions in mind, Rabia is unable to trust men anymore. She confesses that Dervish's question did make her sad, although she does not blame him for that. Rabia needs a nap. Dervish should pray that Rabia goes to sleep. Sometimes one needs a prayer to have a sound sleep.

O Dervish! The month of May is quite scenic for the dwellers along the Canal Bank in Lahore. Winds blow with music announcing the arrival of the summer. Rabia resides along the canal bank, on Canal Street. Although there are not many trees left now, they are enough to embrace the winds of summer and provide a soothing shade. In the evening the scene over the Canal is marvelous. One wishes time would come to a standstill.

These days, numerous underpasses have been built on Canal Bank Road to allow flow of traffic coming from tangent roads. If you stand on any of these underpass bridges, you can see the lines of trees on either side of the canal. The trees seem to be conversing with each other. At times they look as though they are mourning and wailing over the sad demise of their fellows who were slaughtered to widen Canal Bank Road. Sometimes in quiet moments Rabia too joins them. She also recalls her sweet childhood memories, her walks with baba under the trees that no longer exist. Rabia has witnessed the natural wilderness as well as modern materialism dwelling on the old friendly road. She recalls past serenity and solace and sees the present pollution and noise prevailing over this once naturally scenic road. Rabia has witnessed the affection in the eyes of people who once visited the canal bank. Now, she sees the traders everywhere. Few of them are into the business of literature. They are literary Pharaohs of this time. She came across one of them recently. She wishes to narrate the story to Dervish but finds no vigor left for it. Rabia therefore takes her leave of Dervish.

Rab Rakha [God be the protector].

Twelfth Dream

Friendship Should be Guarded Against its Own Dark Sides

19th May 2018

Dervish presents a gift of best wishes to Rabia.

Dervish adores Rabia's personality. It requires courage and patience to fast for sixteen hours. Dervish is watching with the eye of his imagination the scenic surroundings of Rabia's home. He imagines along the canal bank, the lines of trees, the trails and the green belt where people go for strolls. He is thinking about the beautiful scenes created by the tree-tops who whisper to each other in silent moments.

Dervish lives in Whitby, a small town 50 kilometers from Toronto. Whitby is located on the bank of Lake Ontario. Dervish somehow could never develop an affection for the lake because it's too big and seems like an ocean. However Dervish, knows another lake, Lake Scugog, by the town of Port Perry, twenty minutes' drive from Whitby.

For the last few years Dervish is a regular visitor to Lake Scugog. He has passed innumerable afternoons and evenings sitting on its bank under a tree. While sitting there, Dervish wrote a volume of poetry and read many books. Whenever any friend visits Dervish, he takes him or her to see Lake Scugog. Sitting on its bank, Dervish serves the visitor his or her favorite ice cream. If Rabia ever visited Dervish, he would surely take her there and for an ice cream cone. Dervish likes mango and strawberry ice cream. Dervish likes Lake Scugog because he can see its other bank and watch the colorful boats sailing on its smooth blue water. While talking about his favorite lake, Dervish is recalling one of his old poems. He wishes to recite it to Rabia:

The Boats

The innumerable, multicolored and beautiful boats

Sit wondering on the coast

They wait for the lucky day

When they will be freed from the bay

To sail over deep waters to faraway islands

Down the ages the dream princesses dwell on those islands

In a park at the edge of Lake Scugog there is statue of Yousef Palmer. Few people know that the former resident of Port Perry, Yousef Palmer, was the founder of a chiropractic treatment. One of his quotes is inscribed on the statue: "I never considered it beneath my dignity to do anything to relieve human suffering." Whenever Dervish meets a chiropractor who treats aching muscles and joints, he recalls Pakistani wrestlers who besides engaging in the sport of wrestling in the arenas, treat people suffering from joint and muscle aches.

Rabia has asked Dervish about his experience and philosophy of romantic love. Dervish is pleased to tell Rabia that he has been lucky enough to have numerous love affairs. His relationship with women was always that of befriending them. Dervish learnt a lot from women. They played a vital role in his life, turning him into a better poet, writer, therapist, friend and above all a better human being. To clarify his stance, Dervish wishes to narrate to Rabia his own love story.

The story commenced in his university days when he met Bette Davis. Bette was a nurse and Dervish a doctor, but both aspired to become psychotherapists. While working together they became close friends. Dervish had to leave the city, yet their correspondence continued. Bette wanted to become a mother. After three miscarriages she went to Romania to adopt a two-week-old girl. She brought her daughter, Adriana to Newfoundland Canada. Later on they moved to Whitby. Initially Dervish and Bette worked together, then, they also started to live together. After thirteen years' companionship both decided to part ways. At the time of the breakup, Dervish asked Adriana, Sweetheart! I and your Mom will no longer be living together. With whom would you like to live?" Adriana chose to live with Dervish. Bette had no objection to it. Dervish lives in a condo with three bedrooms, one for guests and one each for him and Adriana.

Dervish is happy to tell Rabia that despite their separation Dervish and Bette never exchanged hot words nor had any angry outbursts. They were friends and they are still friends. When Bette and Dervish were separating they asked each other what they have learnt from their friendship. Dervish told Bette he had learnt from her, "Friendship is a cake and the romance is the icing." Bette told Dervish, "You told me once that we don't have to save our friendship from others but from ourselves". Every person has dark as well as a bright side of his personality. A friendship must be saved from the dark side of one's personality so that it does not weaken the bond. That's the reason we still respect each other and despite our breakup we shall remain friends forever. Bette told Dervish, "A few couples remain friends after their separation — we will be one of those lucky couples".

Like Rabia, Dervish also appreciates Khalil Gibran. He likes this saying about love: "Do not ever think you can guide love. If love finds you worthy she will guide you."

As Dervish thinks about love, he recalls a childhood tale. He lived at a place where people did not have water in their homes. They had to fetch water from a nearby river. One day he saw that few of his neighbors were digging. After five feet of digging, the water appeared. Dervish felt very happy for them. But his father told them: "This water contains impurities. You can wash clothes with it but you cannot drink it." The neighbors dug another twenty feet and found more water. My father opined again: "This water is pure, fit for human consumption."

In Dervish's opinion a human heart can have two kinds of love. The first kind of love is shallow love. This love involves jealousy, anger, hatred and bitterness. The second kind is deep love. This love offers peace, tranquility, affection, sincerity and friendship. The majority of humans experience shallow love, and only a small minority experiences the deep love. This minority of lovers are the lucky ones.

Rabia's letter hinted that she wants to tell Dervish a painful story but waits for an opportune moment. Well, Dervish is patient enough to wait for that time. In the famous novel *Siddhartha* by Herman Hesse, when the princess asks Siddhartha, "What have you learnt from years of long meditation and treacherous wandering in the jungles?" Siddhartha replies, "I can wait. I can fast. I can think."

Rabia's creative co-traveler,

Dervish

Thirteenth Dream

What is the Difference Between Sex and Romance?

19th July 2018

Salam to the Foreign Dervish!

Dervish's letter took Rabia to Lake Scugog. Using the colors of nature, she painted a picture of the lake on the canvas of her imagination. Rabia cannot wait to be there and have an ice cream with Dervish. She believes that if she ought to taste the Ice Cream of Scugog, her Creator would take her there. But if He does not will it, she cannot go there despite her earnest efforts. From the experiences of her life so far, Rabia has concluded that getting something or being denied something depends upon the will of God. Most of the things Rabia wished for were denied, yet she was bestowed with much better things that she had never even dreamed of. From that phenomenon, Rabia started to believe in an unknown Power. Rabia longs more to see Lake Scugog than have an ice cream.

Dervish has asked Rabia about her idea of love. Well, the answer had already been given by Dervish in the last letter when he narrated an anecdote that occurred in his childhood. Rabia cannot indulge in a five-foot shallow love. On the other hand, she has not yet found a man who could dive down with her to twenty feet. That's the whole philosophy of Rabia.

Rabia is not going to narrate a painful story to Dervish. Rather she will tell Dervish the ugly experiences of a lonely woman in his homeland. Rabia has reached a state where pains and joys have different meanings altogether. It's the will of God that remains. Whatever must happen will happen regardless of whether it hurts or pleases someone. To Rabia this life is a chain of sorrows and pleasures. Each hardship is followed by a respite and

Dervishes' Inn

vice versa. From Dervish's letter Rabia has deduced that he believes in Khalil Gibran's philosophy of love. To him the connection of both parties should hinge upon friendship. Yet Rabia is interested to know his own philosophy of love based on his personal experiences and observations.

Why? Because Rabia has long been witnessing humans indulging in love, affection, passion and their related agonies. This is a complex facet of life. There is not one quick fix to it. The problem with Rabia is that she cannot talk about such intricate matters with a chaotic mind. She thinks it derogatory to the topic. Rabia has learnt few lessons from life. One of them is: "Respect the words, feelings, images, thoughts and even the pictures made by imagination." Respecting is higher than loving. Respect is a greater magic than love. Love combined with respect is an indispensable magic. It becomes a mind-blowing passion. Love without respect has inbuilt hatred that can erupt into devastating outburst at any time.

Rabia is of the view that love is about being humble. She lives in a society where women are not considered worthy of respect. A woman's sincere feelings have no meaning for a man who is always seeking to defeat her. A woman indulges in love, but man goes for lust, a one-way love, you can say. Sex has also tarnished the image of love. Over here, there is no difference between a friend and a girlfriend. Any relation with a woman must end with sexual intercourse that means nothing more than winning over another female. What a futile exercise. Society has not yet progressed enough to know the difference and respect the difference in the two types of relationships. We are earning degrees not to become civilized, responsible citizens but to get better jobs.

From Rabia's experiences and observations she notes that there are two parts to love: romance and sex. A woman cannot agree to any physical intimacy without the bliss of romance. Before getting into bed a woman wants to spend some time with her partner, talking over a cup of tea, enjoying the weather, going for long drives and listening to few words of appreciation from him about her physical and intellectual beauty. This is her way of romance. A crude advance for sex by the partner annoys her. She doesn't want to act as a sex toy, or a mistress for that matter. Any forced physical pleasure diminishes her urge to make love. A woman can live without love but cannot survive without respect. But no such deprivation occurs in men because they don't make love to engage in romance, rather, they do it to quench their lust. A woman needs romance more than carnal activities. That must be the reason that we find many couples living happily even though the man is not a good performer in bed.

Anyways Rabia will talk in detail in some other letter. This is a sensitive topic that requires more time and concentration of both the mind and the heart. Rabia liked Bette's suggestion: "We should protect our friendship from our own dark sides." Rabia would like to add that if the same care was practiced in every relationship, life would be so beautiful.

O Dervish! Rabia does not fast now. There was a time she was fond of fasting but of late she cannot cope with the thirst. She hopes her Creator will forgive her as He is not an oppressor. To compensate for her transgressions, she prepares delicious meals for the family members who observe this ritual.

O Dervish! Rabia takes her leave.

Fee Aman Allah

Fourteenth Dream

Love, Sex and Marriage

21st May 2018

Dervish says a friendly Salam to Rabia!

Rabia's last letter made Dervish smile for quite a while. He felt as though Rabia has dived deeper into the ocean of human relations. She has been exploring the pearls of various human relations immersed in the ocean of life. Not everybody knows the value of the bond like friendship, romance, love and sex. Those who can find, recognize and value these connections are few and special. Rabia is one of them. This is such a height of intellect where human feelings cannot be expressed in words. Dervish cannot hold back from reciting a relevant verse here:

"Apparently calm water conceals a strange current underneath

What shows a brief affection, is stronger and everlasting indeed"

People with whom Dervish discussed sex life during his professional and social life can be divided into three types. He denotes them with 3R's. The first "R" stands for "Reproduction". These are traditional couples who wish to become parents. They use sex to produce children. The second "R" is for "Relationship. Couples in this group are in love with each other, however they do not use sex to produce children. They believe that having sex is a physical manifestation of their loving relationship. The third "R" denotes "Recreation". These couples are mostly found in the West. To them engaging in a sexual relationship is more of a pleasure like watching a movie or eating a hamburger.

Dervish also met couples who in various phases of their life experimented with various facets of sex. Their values and preferences about love, friendship and sex have been changing all along. Dervish has his own opinion: "Any sane adult couple, man-woman, two men or two women, have the full right to engage in any kind of mutually agreed romantic relationship."

Dervish's own voyage of love, romance and sex was quite complex and cumbersome, not narrate-able in a few words. He was born and raised in the East under a thick umbrella of religious and moral values. But when he landed in the West, he endeavored to understand human relations through perspective of psychology instead of morality. Dervish has always strove to respect women. He has many female friends. Most of them have remained his friends throughout his life.

A few months ago, one of his old friends left a message to call her. When Dervish called back, she told him that she suffers from terminal cancer and has only a few months in this world. She had decided to see her old friends. Dervish was one of them. When Dervish went to see her, she met him with the same old warmth. Dervish felt so happy to know that the old friend remembered him after so many years.

Through his professional and romantic experiences Dervish has reached certain conclusions "Men and women have a different psychology. Many women wish to have romantic discourse before getting into sexual intercourse, whereas many men want to have sex before embarking upon the journey of romance and love.

While living in the West, Dervish observed that the West has accepted "dating". Most parents urge their young sons or daughters to have multiple friendships. They think this gives them ample opportunity to know their preferences and make an informed and wise decision about their life partners. They don't want their offspring to marry their "first date". Whereas the dwellers of the East follow the single line of their favorite poet, *Faraz*:

Ham mohabbat mein bhi Toheed kay qaail hein Faraz...

O Faraz! In love affair too, we believe in oneness...

Since the East has not yet accepted dating, young people remain unaware of the pleasures of dating before marriage. In the East, friendship, love, sex and children are integral parts of a package called "marriage". In the West, people can enjoy each of these relations separately.

In the West, Dervish met many couples living together without marriage as well as couples who got married but did not produce children. There are also many unmarried mothers in the West. Dervish knows many men and women who remarried after divorcing their first spouse and whose second marriage was happier than the first.

Another pleasant thing about West is that, people respect others' decisions. Unlike in the East, people in the West pay no heed to "what other people would think". They make conscious decisions using their own judgment. The best thing about their decisions is that they take full responsibility for their choices. They do not blame God or their relatives for their problems.

Dervish confesses that despite the long letter, he has not been able to express his point of view as he had wished to. Nevertheless, this is his first effort.

As the evening of life drifts into the compound of his heart, a feeling that 'all relationships in life are temporary', surrounds Dervish. He dares to say:

"This is an age of relationship - recession

Any enduring relationship is a great possession"

With this, Rabia's overseas Dervish friend takes leave of her.

Dervishes' Inn

Fifteenth Dream

Dating is Just an Exchange of Physical Pleasure and Anxiety...

21ˢᵗ May 2018

O Dervish! Please accept a Salam from Lahore.

Dervish's observations gave immense pleasure to Rabia. It's a pleasant feeling to know that two creative minds have a beautiful symmetry of views despite living poles apart. If Dervish feels that he could not complete his argument in the last letter, Rabia would like him to finish his narration in the next.

It may surprise Dervish that the society and culture is not the same as that which he left decades ago. Though not yet accepted as a social norm, in Rabia's society dating is a common feature now. There are two kinds of dating — for fun and for money. Dating for fun is also a status symbol and an acceptable norm in upper classes of society. But there is a dichotomy. Even in the upper classes men like to flirt with others' daughters and sisters, but do not like their women to date other men. This is also used as a weapon to exploit those women for the rest of their lives. Dating for money has various forms. Rabia will dilate upon them in ensuing paragraphs.

Every year Valentine's Day is celebrated with more zeal and enthusiasm than in the West. One man presents Valentine's Day gifts to numerous women on that day. The same is done by the women. But all this is done in a covert manner. Dating has been accepted as a last resort to address suffocation, frustration and perversion. There is no role for the mind or soul. It's causing more damage to people's psyche because our society is not civilized. Such unions do give some physical pleasure to both but bring with them guilt and anxiety. It is not done to seek a life partner but for some diversion. Materialistic trends have also accentuated the culture of extra marital relations. It hurts Rabia to say that dating couple most of the time exploit each other's weaknesses. The women display their beauty and the men their wealth. Rabia opines that the dating couples who meet for pleasure, peace and bliss, bring home anxiety and frustration.

Rabia thinks that intentions and attitudes also emit waves. If you visit certain place you pick up an aura of either negative or positive energy. Such energy does affect your psyche. Modern day scientists call it the journey of time and space. The conception and romance of s soul mate is nothing more than a myth. Society has induced filthy fumes of sex in the minds of men and women alike. Fumes have turned into clouds and these are getting thicker and thicker. Whatever they watch in the porn movies they endeavor to do in real life. The rigorous use of body organs is called true love and real pleasure. Such futile exercises are causing many physical and psychological disorders. People of this society are addicted to extremes, whether freedom or confinement. Our society must undergo many cultural tremors. It might take a toll on a few generation before it transforms into a civilized one.

Over here as well, Rabia had a chance to meet innumerable men and women who had been in relationships with their counterparts. It's heartening to know that everyone claimed that he or she was deeply in love with their partner. Amongst them were certain individuals who were married as well while others were not. To them the rigor of a physical relationship is what they call "love". Many men proudly talk about having relationships with the maximum number of women, as if they were stallions.

Rabia takes it as a "male-complex". As a psychiatrist what has Dervish to say about it? To Rabia, this sense of domination in men is an incurable sickness, nothing to do with reality. Rabia has met women who boasted about their sexy figure their whole life. They told bedroom stories, about how skillfully they had been quenching men's lust in a variety of ways. At the end of the day Rabia saw such women marrying men who did not bother much about sex. Rabia also came across many women who married big mill owners or retired officers for their fortunes. They also complained about not finding a soul mate. Rabia felt that the men-women relation in her society revolves around wealth or at best infatuation. Love is different altogether. It demands consistency, patience and sacrifice. Only a soul mate can do all that. Such people are successful indeed.

Very few people find their soul mates as this society has not yet been able to progress beyond initial psycho-social barriers. They have time neither to understand nor look for a soul mate. The attraction towards your soul mate is like a gravitational pull. Despite being a hundred miles apart, the soul mates feel as though they are peacefully infusing into each other. Having acquired your soul mate, the feeling towards another never occurs. It's like tasting the fruits of Heaven. After that you don't feel like eating earthly fruits. Finding your soul mate is the journey of solace. On the contrary, the seekers of lust who connect for pitiful gains remain ever perturbed. It might happen consciously or unconsciously but, in either case, there is metal sounding, warning them of approaching danger. But few people heed it.

O Dervish! Rabia's well of life is full of observations, experiments and analysis. She can divide it into three phases. Rabia's first love was her father but she was equally attached to her uncles. She smells her Baba's fragrance when she's around her uncles. The elder Uncle Anwar Ali was reticent and yet soft-spoken. Rabia never heard him backbiting. He could recite Punjabi poetry in a much sweeter accent than in the Saraiki language. His recitations were very impressive. I learnt effective communication skills from my uncle Anwar Ali.

My Uncle Noshad was a military man. Survivor of two wars, Uncle Noshad had too many secrets in his heart. Such secrets make someone polite and reserve. The effect of his experiences and secrets was evident in his few comments. Rabia always saw him immersed in his deep thoughts. But whenever he spoke about art literature and politics, it was marvelous. He used to tell stories from his military life. Long story sessions, over tea and coffee made the nights pass quickly. Rabia enjoyed listening to his philosophy of life at such tender age.

Then there were five more uncles younger than Uncle Anwar Ali. Working in the accounting office of a department was Uncle Imtiaz Ali. A simple soul and staunch follower of God and the Prophet PBUH, he was a living example of simplicity. Uncle Afzaal was another gem of a person. He never complained about his relatively tough life. Last but not the least was uncle Saleem, an important member of the National Hockey Team and renowned participant in the Hockey Olympics and the World Cup. Chachoo Farooq and Chachoo Khalid were two other pearls in the rosary of my uncles. Life went on with all its ups and downs as it is a beautiful mix of sorrows and pleasures.

O Dervish! Rabia had a chance to work with an NGO and an opportunity to interview hundreds of men and women coming from various walks of life and a variety of rural and urban backgrounds. Which help her better understand the psychological patterns of men, women and society. The compilation of her anthology: *Afsana Asr e Hazir Mein* [Short Story of the Present Era] provided Rabia another opportunity to interact with hundreds of writers. It further broadened her frame of observation. Compiling the above referred encyclopedia was a unique experience and a blessed opportunity for

Rabia. Rabia wished to live life in certain manner but life offered something altogether different but good. That is the whole story of Rabia's life.

Coming back to the man-woman relationship, now with mutual consent a physical relationship is possible even over here. The only difference is that there are many strings of interests attached to the relationship besides seeking the mutual pleasure. Men are also allowed to rape their wives, when they sleep with them. *Toheed* (Monotheism) in love, is nothing more than a wish or a dialogue. *Toheed* requires us to perish but we are in the race of survival. In the race to survival, our society has gone through a paradigm shift. Come around sometime, live here for few days and observe what you left decades ago. Rabia believes only Zuleika was the true follower of "Monotheism in love." Her passion and love for one — Yousef — has been praised by some historians and criticized by others. Rabia has a different opinion here: "If you wish to be loved by someone like Zuleika, you have to be Yousef in first place." He would not have been Yousef, had he been lured by beauty, lust, wealth, kingdom, or petty gains. Only a brave individual can refuse such glamour. Yousef is Rabia's ideal, her first love. She has dedicated all her books to him. If you wish to understand it, do please see Rabia's books.

With the mention of her first and enduring love, Rabia says Fi Amman Allah [In God's protection] to Dervish as the battery of the cellular phone is about to die. Dawn is breaking here. In the far distance someone is playing a flute. At times, some crazy person sits by the canal bank to blow out his pain through the morning air.

Two stars were supposed to meet tonight but the night has already passed. The day is about to appear but Rabia is saddened by the daylight.

Dervishes' Inn

Sixteenth Dream

Men's Madonna / Whore Complex

23rd May 2018

Adaab!

Dervish had heard many people say: "After forty the humans do not experience new things. Only old experiences repeat themselves, turning life into a boring routine. After forty, the poets, writers and artists suffer from a creative menopause and often recite their friend - Iqbal's famous verse:

Khuda tujhay Kisi toofaN say ashna kar dey

Kay teray behar ki maujoN mein iztrab NahiN

God may confront you with a tempest storm

Tides of your ocean shouldn't be still and calm

Notwithstanding, Dervish opines that a new experience is mandatory for the evolution and survival of any poet, writer or artist who reaches this age. In the evening of his life, meeting with Rabia and this meaningful exchange of letters is considered by Dervish a new creative experience.

Since Rabia and Dervish are now friends, Dervish would like to make a literary confession. He wishes to tell Rabia the story of his two beloveds. When he lived in the East his first beloved was Urdu. He used to write poetry, short stories and novelettes in Urdu, it would keep his beloved happy. But when he moved to the West, English made him her friend. His new friendship annoyed Urdu. She wrote a letter of grievance to Dervish. Here, Dervish would like to share few sentences from her letter:

"O my veteran beloved, my poet, my writer! Perhaps you have forgotten about me, but I still remember each, and

every moment passed with you. I carry all the sweet memories of our companionship, our love and our friendship. My name is Urdu. On landing in the West, you got on friendly terms with English as you wrote articles in it. In the beginning I thought English was your professional need. Since you had always desired to become a psychotherapist, a messiah who would treat afflicted hearts and serve humanity, I was happy for you. Then I realized that like all Eastern beloveds, I too was a simple soul. Your interaction with English went beyond a working relation. She had become your beloved. First you wrote psychological articles in English, then you wrote poems and created some beautiful short stories as well. My heart burned when someone translated your English short story into Urdu. Since that day, I have been jealous of English. I felt like grabbing English by her hair and eating her raw; but when my anger subsided, I realized that I had no right to curse English. She was a stranger, an alien. If at all I must express my grievance to anyone, it was you. You are my love, you abandoned me and befriended English. You cast me out of your heart and started to write in English."

Dervish feels thankful to Rabia as she emotionally connected him back to his angry "ex", Urdu. The exchange of dreams is a novel creative experience for him.

Rabia has asked a question of Dervish and she requires him to answer it as psychologist. Well, the brief reply is that Dervish has met many men who suffer from the Madonna or Whore Complex. Men with this ailment have two extremes in their attitude. If they deeply respect a woman, they are unable to have a romantic or sexual relationship with her. On the other hand, if such men establish a physical connection with certain woman, they do not respect her, rather they consider her a whore or prostitute. In both cases they do not see women as human. Such people cannot become friends, companions or life partners of women. They require psychotherapy.

Dervish has deeply reflected upon and always appreciated Yousef-Zuleikha as mythological characters of

Middle East — especially Yousef, as he could interpret dreams. Being a psychotherapist, Dervish has always taken keen interest in the interpretation of dreams. Dervish also agrees with Rabia that we as civilization are passing through an interim phase of evolution. Many man-woman relationships are nothing more than teenage relations in the thrall of emotion and lacking wisdom. It seems as if countless people although having grown physically adult remain intellectually immature.

Rabia's mental maturity has always impressed Dervish. He wonders how one could be so mature at such age. Is it heredity, family grooming or her own sheer hard work that has granted her such wisdom? Although Rabia is a down to earth person in her behavior yet Dervish thinks that many people especially the men must be intimidated by her cognitive maturity.

Reading of Rabia's letters is also helping Dervish in understanding her short stories. He is optimistic that one day these letters will be recognized by readers and critics as innovative creations. Rabia's short stories are unique in the sense that they are simultaneously connected to the conscious and the subconscious mind. If we think of her short stories as paintings, then these letters provide the frame for those paintings.

Immersed in the flow of consciousness Dervish was absorbed into writing this letter oblivious of the clock that has just clicked 12 pm. Unlike Rabia, Dervish has yet not acquired the "divine insight" that would keep him awake all night, busy in creative worship and reflecting upon the mysteries of the Universe. He loves to sleep instead, as he loves to dream.

Dervish a sinner, a chronic sinner, begs to take leave of Rabia.

Seventeenth Dream

Hard to Say, Harder to Endure

23rd May 2018

In a blessed morning of Ramadan, Rabia presents her Salam to Dervish!

Awesome! I can only wish that the men here too could find the beloveds like the ones befriended by Dervish. That could take sex out of their minds and put that energy in their bodies. In that way the country might take a faster leap forward.

Rabia read Dervish's last letter twice. One sentence made her happy as well as sad. It was not a sentence but a question. Rabia has been looking for its answer all her life. Now as she enters the afternoon of her life, she finds herself as clueless as ever. There was something that prevented her from living a normal life like other girls. She did find a blurred answer but did not accept it. Perhaps Dervish has found the answer in his analysis. She declines to fully accept that as well. It is against her temperament. She takes it as self-praise or boasting. Rabia admits that she was a common girl. The journey and the talent of creativity might have been the reward of her seclusion and the solitude imposed upon her by the environment. Rabia takes it as a precious gift of her Creator. She has never imagined acquiring such blessings. In other words, when all other paths were closed the train of life chose this track.

Now to Dervish's other question. Dervish, I know, would digest the answer but Rabia does not know others' reaction. 'It is hard to say and harder to endure.'

O Dervish! You are right. It happened like that and it is still like that. Men and women both are victims of such situations. It is Rabia's attribute or may be a shortcoming, she does not know; but due to that reason she could not live the normal life, she had always wished for. She endeavored to live a normal life but could not. Then she accepted the truth that it was not for her and her reward was not a normal life. Everyone is made to a different formula. I agree with Rumi: *"All creative minds suffer from the similar dilemma. Woman is a ray of God. She is not earthly beloved. She is creative not created."*

Due to the above mentioned painful fact, there is a void in Rabia's life. She preferred seclusion over the charms of privacy. Her decision was driven by the love of Yousef who preferred to go to prison rather indulging into the pleasures of an illicit relationship. In the solitude of prison, the window to the heart opens. Such meditation creates hope, the hope of light and awareness. No matter how long the night is, it is followed by a bright morning.

It may be called an attribute or a shortcoming but Rabia has endured pains and losses due to her habit of not indulging with men. She still observes sea of life while standing on its shore. She is surprised as well as hopeful. The small girl inside Rabia at times turns away from the rhetoric of life. In a trance by herself she wishes to drench herself with the rain on a hillside. She has never desired any man to peep into her innocent heart. She knows that he wouldn't be able to get along with her. He would simply be astonished at her way of life. She is quite sure that nobody would enter her life. If he were to, he would either turn her into temple or trample her into the dust. In any case Rabia wishes not to turn into any of these. She desires to stay an ordinary person.

The question is so cumbersome that despite her best effort, some part has to be left unaddressed. Rabia is not just a body available to be conquered by another person. To her the body is of not much significance. At the same time, she attaches an importance to her physical self and cannot allow it to play freely. She wants her clay-made body to infuse into another similar body. By this she wishes to fade away. Now Rabia has given up the search of origin of her clay. That too is a tall order. She just watches the life around her that is nothing more than children's play place. In the words of uncle *Ghalib*:

"Through the day and the night

I enjoy the amusement of life"

She remains vigilant all the time. She knows who she is. What is the real depth of such and such a person and their extent of access? Who is sitting on a heap of wealth by which he wishes to win over whom? Rabia quietly watches all, the silence has its own language. To sum up, when the divine bell above seven skies ring, Rabia is into another trance. She feels as if she neither exists physically nor otherwise yet she can listen to the silence that speaks to her.

O Dervish! Now let us talk about the inertia after forty years. Rabia tends to disagree with the connotation that an inertia takes over a person as he reaches forty. She thinks that the real beauty of life, the real beauty of experiences, the real beauty of observations, bloom like a fresh flower after forty. But to attain that you must have a clear direction, positive thinking, an open mind endeavoring for love and peace. Then every riddle of life is visible to you as in a revelation, an intuition or a dream. This happens without any meditation. This is, rather, a reward of past meditations. On the contrary if you are a materialistic person who believes in his own struggle and is arrogantly proud of himself, then the inertia takes over. The person has no new experiences and does not get the opportunity for new observations. Such people are like a candle flickering to its end. Such people need psychiatric help. The majority of people are like that. The other group is in the minority. After forty they become precious like diamonds.

O Dervish! You must have observed that youth is always intoxicating, and the real beauty of a person comes out after forty.

Before asking for a leave, Rabia wishes to once again quiz Dervish. Every man wants to become father of a child. It's only natural. Why did this instinctive urge never take over Dervish? Rabia even now has the urge to become a mother. A mother is also one form of a creator. But a woman must remember that she can create but cannot change the lineage of genes. The importance and force of genes is significant. It ultimately takes over and manifests its reality. The dawn is smiling, dreams sleeping and another day about to arrive. Rabia would like to sleep now. Like Dervish, she does not dream every day but whatever she dreams is very soothing for her.

Good morning O Dervish.

Eighteenth Dream

Silence…Solitude…Wisdom

25th May 2018

Good evening to Rabia!

Having read Rabia's letter Dervish reflected for a while. Then he firmly concluded that she has dived into the deep waters of awareness. Very deep, where the swimmer's feet cannot touch the bottom. In that state, either people drown or they start swimming. Rabia was lucky. She is swimming in the deep waters of awareness. As well, she climbed the heights of cognitive peaks, then took a flight of imagination. Now she is flying into the space of dreams.

Dervish is fast realizing that if he wants to keep up pace with his creative co-traveler, he must learn to swim into the deep waters of awareness and take the highest flight of thoughts. Only that can safeguard their creative friendship. Without two-way discourse, these letters would turn into a monologue. Suffice it to say, dialogue is the building block of any sincere friendship. In Dervish's view, lucky are those men and women who bind themselves into the knot of friendship. He prefers friendship over love, sexual relations and marriage. These relations can tarnish the elegance, innocence and spontaneity of friendship.

In Dervish's life, his friends have played an important role. In Canada, his likeminded friends have established a Dervishes' Inn for intellectual discourse and creative dialogue. Dervish writers, poets and artists coming from other cities and countries are invited to this platform. If Rabia ever visited Canada, Dervish would take her to the Inn. He would first introduce her to other Dervishes, then request her to read one of her *Afsanas*

Dervishes' Inn

[short stories] on the fora. An *Afsana* which would simultaneously touching the conscious and the subconscious. It would be followed by an open discussion over the meaning of the story. Dervish is clear that a genuine poet, writer, scholar or philosopher is essentially a Dervish inside.

Rabia has inquired why Dervish did not produce children or start a family. In reply, Dervish wants to share two important incidents of his life with her. Dervish was only ten when his father, Abdul Basit, who was an atheist, suffered a psychological trauma. After one year as he healed from that trauma, he turned into a Sufi. Relatives opined that his father had undergone a nervous breakdown. However, my father firmly believed that he has undergone a spiritual breakthrough. Dervish thinks this childhood incident must have motivated him to become a psychotherapist. When Dervish realized that mental ailments could be hereditary, he decided not to marry or produce children to prevent the transfer of mental disorder to next generation.

Right from his youth, Dervish realized that his maternal relatives were loving, traditional and religious, whereas his paternal side was unreligious and non-traditional. Dervish was twenty when he revealed to his uncle Arif Abdul Mateen that after years of pondering, he has said goodbye to God and religion. His uncle smiled and replied: "Son! Every nation has two groups of people in it, the traditional and creative. The first group is in majority and follows highway of tradition. The second minority group does not follow the conventional path, they rather follow the trail of their heart. All poets and philosophers, scientists and scholars, writers and mystics, reformers and revolutionaries belong to the second group. This group has certain ideals. The people of this group pay a heavy price to follow them. You belong to the same minority group."

Dervish in his very youth realized that if he lived in his traditional eastern society, he could be killed, sent to jail, go insane or commit suicide. In view of the circumstances, Dervish in his youth made two decisions. He would not start a family and he would no longer live in the traditional society of the East. Therefore, one fine morning he stuffed a few clothes and books into a suitcase and left for an unknown destination. While writing all this Dervish is recalling the first verse of his life, not included in any of his books:

"I was lonely, am lonely, and wish to live lonely

I wish to dwell in the realm of solitude, always lonely."

The solitude is very dear to Dervish. In that solitude he has read and written numerous books. Now he knows that there is a strong relation between silence, seclusion and wisdom. After arriving and settling in the West, Dervish from his observations, reading, experience and analysis encountered another mystery of life: "There is a hairline difference between insanity, creativity and spirituality." Dervish can expand upon the topic some other time if Rabia wishes.

Dervish would like to know whether Rabia's maternal or paternal family ever produced a poet, writer, scholar or philosopher. Or did any one of those ever suffer from any psychological issue?

Since Dervish came to this awareness, he has treated innumerable people with the psychological disorders so that they can live a normal life. Dervish has named his clinic CREATIVE PSYCHOTHERAPY CLINIC. Dervish now believes that creative works contribute to mental health.

O Rabia! The night is half gone here. Dervish must rise in the morning to treat many distressed hearts. He therefore says goodnight to Rabia.

Nineteenth Dream

Man is an Action, Woman a Reaction!

25th May 2019

O Dervish Rabia greets you!

Birds are chirping. The dark blue sky is turning into a lighter one to receive the sun that prepares to cast its burning heat, despite returning from a land where it must have showered its cool brightness.

Rabia has just finished Dervish's letter. She has received the replies to her questions like a laboratory report, accurate and complete. Rabia believes in genetic codes. She observes that genes have a lot to play in one's life. Despite the effects of the environment, education and grooming in one's life, genes do manifest in each phase of life. Present day medical research has proved that genetic engineering does alter the pattern of one's life.

Rabia however wishes to ask a man about Dervish's theory in the emotional context. She wants to ask whether Dervish feels any emotional pain (about not having children due to the genetic issue). No? Yes?

Rabia agrees with Dervish's concept of majority and minority groups. From her own observations, she concluded the same. Rabia's family did not produce any published writer, yet she saw many people in her clan who adored art and literature. Her father tells her that her grandmother was a poetess. She died young due to a mysterious disease. All of her poetry is contained in the letters that she wrote to her beloved husband with whom she lived for only four years. Rabia's ancestors came from the Pink City of Jaipur - Rajhistan. The city lives for the arts. Pink is a symbol of romance and romance is an art. Rabia's favorite color is also pink. Art is nothing but organizing things into a certain sequence. It is sophistication. Inner sophistication takes the art out of a person; otherwise inner truths are similar with everyone.

Reading books was an ancestral hobby in Rabia's family. The books were handed down. Her great grandfather, Hashem Ali Khan was a college graduate in those days when there were only a few colleges in the Subcontinent. Her grandfather Kazim Ali Khan was a learned man too. In those days an educated man was forced to find a job in the British Government, so he did that. Grandfather had a flare for poetry, perhaps due to his wife. Their four-year companionship focused on poetry only. Whenever he came across a good verse he copied into his diary. His diary was a precious gift to Rabia. As written earlier, Rabia's elder grandmother Akhtar Begum was a poetess. Whenever she wrote a letter to her husband she wrote many couplets, which she also recorded in her diary. Now Rabia realizes the height of sensitivity of those feelings expressed in poetry, especially when soon after marriage her husband had to go to another city, and they were unable to meet. The longing for love must have been translated into verses of poetry. Physical expression of love was considered out of place in those days, however, poetry might have become a vehicle of communication between the couple. The words must have pierced into her soul. One day they took her to her final abode. The untimely departure of a beautiful wife must have turned my grandfather into a poet. Rabia's observation says: "A *distanced relationship is an unnatural one.*"

My second grandmother Nafeesa Begum was a cousin of the first one. My grandfather's relationship with his second wife was an ideal one. For his entire life he took care of her with utmost respect. Respect keeps a woman young and glued to her husband. Motherhood never comes between the couple. She too remained fresh, sophisticated and graceful till the end. That was the time of writing letters; email, messaging and cellphones emerged later. Grandma used to regularly write letters to the children of family and relatives. She would make sure to reply to their letters as soon as possible. She never missed sending Eid cards as well. She wrote in wonderful prose. That too was in the times when traditions did not permit the education of women in the subcontinent. All the females in her family had received basic education. They not only wrote well but also spoke Urdu with its proper accent. Rabia followed them but could not fully adopt their Urdu accent.

Right from her childhood Rabia had idealized her grandmother Nafeesa Begum. She was a decent and graceful lady. Soft spoken, passionate and a loving soul, Nafeesa Begum was never seen angry or shouting at domestic servants. She was neither arrogant nor proud. Generous by nature, Grandma was never heard backbiting or using bad words. She was a fragrant plant of love whose perfume had spread and kept everything alive and fresh. Rabia learnt a lot from her grandma.

Rabia's father was a writer and a painter. In the beginning he wrote under the name of Manno Selani, then he wrote translations for children. Later he took to painting. He made marvelous paintings. Baba was very possessive and sensitive about his painting room. Once a pet dog entered the room and spoiled his work. Thinking that it was done by his sister, he punished her. She was the only sister of eight siblings. She is visiting Rabia nowadays and intends to leave tomorrow. Rabia feels as if she is parting with her daughter.

Rabia's ancestors' professions were government service and the forces. Arts was not chosen as a profession but stayed as an essential part of their style and life. However, times are changing now. Creativity was never ancestral with Rabia. Rabia takes it as the Creator's gift. Like other aspects of her life, if nature had shown her the end before the beginning, what would poor Rabia have done? Nothing much. Or even now if her would-be life partner snatches this away, she would have no choice but to accept. At times such oppression give, birth to new stories.

O Dervish! Rabia saw a dream when she was thirteen. She shared it with no one. Again, in the beginning of this year she saw the same dream. Now she has understood. It hinted to her that she belongs to the minority group of people, the same people who follow their heart and not the prevailing customs and traditions. Now she has concluded that whatever happened in her life, was bound to happen because of her belonging to the minority group. All relations, pains and pleasures are in fact reactions to certain actions. Rabia's observations tell her that: "Man is action and woman a reaction." They both are action and reactions in all facets of their relationship. After forty, this action-reaction phenomenon either gets intensified or smoothens out. The "reaction" part usually becomes non-reactive and soft. That's the beauty of the relationship. But if it does not happen, it leads to a miserable end.

O Dervish! The light of the day is spreading all around. In Uncle Arif Mateen's words: "The next day is calling out the majority group..." But Rabia is overwhelmed by sleep and wishes to embrace her slumber. She wishes to have a sound sleep now.

Good night and good morning.

O Dervish! Love to all Dervishes of the universe. Love is like a fragrance. If it is true it spreads all around.

Goodbye.

Twentieth Dream

A Little Person

18th May 2018

Salam to Dervish's overseas friend!

Dervish is watching out of his cottage. Out there, a few clouds are playing hide and seek in the sky. Only two weeks back, a heavy thunder-snowstorm broke down many trees and houses in the vicinity. But now the temperature is rising, and the summer season is slowly making its way to the city. Canada is a country where the temperature drops to minus 30 C in December and rises to plus 30 C in June. If Canada were a human, we would easily diagnose him as a sufferer of bipolar disorder. The weather changes in Canada are so abrupt that we feel as if we are living in different countries in different months.

O Rabia! Dervish once again strives to offer a detailed reply to your pointed question. Dervish has adored women, befriended women, loved them, romanced them and enjoyed beautiful days and nights with them, but never wished to produce children or start a family. He didn't want to become a father. He likes children but never wanted to have his own kids. His only sister Amber once asked Dervish: "Why don't you have your own children?" He replied: "Two children out of your four children are mine." Amber had smiled at his reply.

It was a blissful coincidence that Amber's two elder kids Afifa and Urooj stayed with her in the East but the two younger ones, Wardah and Zeeshan came to Dervish in the West. All his life, Dervish enjoyed acting as maternal Uncle. Two years back, Wardah gave birth to Aliza. Out of love Dervish calls her Mona Liza. Last week, I took Wardah and Mona Liza to McDonalds. That evening was full of love and rejoicing. Dervish is of the view that all children belong to all of us. That is the reason Adriana who was adopted by Bette Davis still lives with him. In this way Dervish can say that he acted as a father all along but never became a father physically. Adriana calls him a friendly father. Dervish reproduces his own verse for this occasion:

"It doesn't matter who brought those kids into this world

Symbols of a hopeful tomorrow, they belong to whole world"

He hopes he has answered Rabia's question.

Having read about Rabia's grandmother, Dervish was reminded of his own. His grandmother Sarwar lived at 4 - *Mazang Road Lahore*. Dervish used to visit her every year along with his mother Ayesha and sister Amber. Dervish had great affection for his Naani. Her habit that touched him the most was, she always asked Dervish his choice:-

"Son! What would you like drink, juice or milk? "Milk", Okay, would you like it cold or warm?" "Cold", Okay, would you like it with ice?" "Son! Would you like to sleep in the bedroom on the roof?" "I will sleep on roof with my Naani Amma," I used to reply. She would always address children like little people. From his Naani Amma, Dervish learnt to respect children and value their opinion. That is why Dervish respects boys and girls. Respect is the first step towards love. Like Rabia's grandmother, Dervish's Naani was also an ocean of love.

From Rabia's letters she seems attached to spirituality. Dervish is curious to know whether Rabia ever met a saint, sadhu or a Sufi. Or whether Rabia ever underwent a spiritual experience? Dervish requests a leave from Rabia as he is invited over for lunch with Adriana and her boyfriend Georgie in an Iranian restaurant, Zaffron. Dervish is lucky that he is not residing in a country where he would be labeled an infidel and punished for having lunch in Ramadan.

Twenty-First Dream

Bells of the Hearts Ring!

26th May 2018

Rabia presents her Salam from the East!

It's already morning over here. The pleasant breeze is blowing. Its intoxicating scent is pervading everywhere. Rabia thanks Dervish who cheerfully answers her pointed and annoying questions. Rabia is fully aware that had she asked such questions of a common person, he would have scolded her and refused to continue. Above all, he would have gossiped here, there and everywhere. The foremost attribute of a Dervish is that he holds in himself high esteem and values perseverance. Such higher attributes can be seen in the discourse between the historical characters of Rabia Basri and Hassan Basri. Such depth is also found with Mansur Hallaj. What an irony! Today the dervishes of a materialistic world talk about the great Saints of their times.

It's nice to know that two women, his maternal grandmother and Bette Davis, played important roles in the journey of Dervish's search for wisdom. He wrote in one of his previous letters about his farewell conversation with Bette Davis. On asking what she learned from a twenty-five years friendship with Dervish, she replied: "The friendship is so precious that we should protect it from ourselves. Every individual has bright as well as dark side of his or her personality. The dark side of one's personality can harm the friendship." Bette had understood that life is a mystery, it should be guarded against the dark attributes. The men who never have come across a wise woman, feel a void in their life, but they cannot express it. The masculine ego keeps men away from the path of wisdom.

On reading about Dervish's grandmother, Rabia recalls her own.

Whereas Rabia's paternal family was decent enough, her maternal family was more loving and traditional. They lived in the old "Walled City" of Lahore, steeped in its centuries-old culture. They are open-hearted happy people who speak exuberantly. They practice their own religious values not enforced by any priest or cleric. There were numerous shrines in the vicinity and these people were caretakers of their saints buried there. They paid homage to the shrines on happy as well as gloomy occasions. In this way, the poor and needy were also fed. Though fierced in their love and hatred, these folks do not carry grudges. There is no place in their heart for a long-term rivalry. Those big-hearted, food loving and merry folks of the old city would find an occasion to get together to eat and talk together. So Rabia was raised in two opposite cultures who had altogether different ideals, traditions and customs.

Dervish has asked a secret question. The secrets should remain a secret, but Rabia would endeavor to answer it. Rabia had a desire to visit some saint, sadhu or mystic but never found an opportunity. Nevertheless, here Rabia would like to share with Dervish a mystic experience. The incident was like a dream-reality phenomenon. It happened much earlier than her admission into Government College Lahore. No university was admitting her in to graduate program due to a typographical error in her result card. In those days she found an opportunity to visit a calligraphy exhibition. Yunas Majid was showcasing his paintings on Qur'anic verses. Realizing Rabia's problem he advised her to visit the shrine of Ghazi Elam Deen Shaheed and offer the prayers on the tomb. She did so the very next day. On the following night she had a dream that "she was climbing a hill on a rainy day." One year later she was climbing the same hill and as by coincidence it was a rainy day. She was granted admission into Government College Lahore. She never had imagined that she would become a Ravian.

Another selfless and elegant mystic who moved Rabia is Irfan Ul Haque. The meeting with him was a beautiful coincidence. It was the period when Rabia was mentally perturbed to an indescribable extent. It was the Islamic month of Meraj, the month of the meeting of the Beloved Prophet PBUH with Almighty Allah that had made the universe halt for a while. The event has so many secrets in it. If we understand that we might be able to know the secrets of lovingness and the value of respect in the affairs of Love with God.

When she reached him, it was early morning. The cool breeze was blowing. She was in still in the trance of having paced the canal bank. There was freshness, peace and silence all over. Life had taken Rabia out of time and space. On reaching his home, she crossed a large compound only to find a big gathering in a circular white hall. Since it was month of Mearaj, the lovers and lovers of the Prophet PBUH had gathered there in a large number to hear the miraculous occurrence of Mearaj. Irfan Sahib was expounding upon those parts of the historical incident of Mearaj that are generally missed out. He was offering his point of view: The great incident of Mearaj teaches us an important lesson of regard for your guest. We boost about the fleet of cars, our own and others' alike. We tell people, "Look I invited so and so, and he arrived at my place in a late-model luxury vehicle." This is not the way to pay respect to the guest of honor. Look at God, when he invited Prophet PBUH to the heavens to have a dialogue, he sent his best conveyance to pick as well as drop off his beloved guest. This is the manifestation of the climax of honor for an honorable guest.

Irfan Sahib had arrived in Lahore only the previous day. He was staying with Maraub Sahib in Muslim Town.

Uncle Zafar had called Rabia to visit there. She had heard that Irfan Sahib does not meet women. When Rabia arrived there she found herself the one woman in the male gathering. But since she had spoken to Irfan Sahib before, there was no chance of an awkward situation. The food had been served already. While a few people were discussing their personal problems with Irfan Sahib, the others paid their respects and tributes to him. The crowd was gradually thinning out. Then Irfan Sahib suddenly got up and took a seat beside her. He sat there for a while in utter silence. Rabia felt as if the Dervishes bring with them their aura. She felt enveloped in his spiritual zone. There were two Faqeers sitting together, not a man and a woman.

After a while, Rabia started sweating as if she were wrapped in warm clothes. Then her soaked body started to shiver under her attire. She felt as if her all energy was leaving her body through her feet. Someone brought a cup of green tea. When she received it, she saw her hand trembling. Then she felt a severe chill. It was the first time in her life that she had experienced this phenomenon.

Rabia wanted to ask many questions of Irfan Sahib but all questions had suddenly vanished from her mind. A complaint cum question that she asked from on the telephone was this: "Despite all her hard work, why has the life not been fair to her?" Irfan sahib had remembered the question. He moved his passionate hand over her head and spoke: "At times we just ask for candies, but the Giver has something big to offer." That was the outcome of her stray visions. After that there was serenity. The paper-faces around had unveiled. She could see everything with more clarity. She felt herself sitting on an easy chair on the highest mountain, all the world under her feet. Now when Rabia glances back at her past she concludes that life is full of mysteries. The closed environment wherein Rabia was raised could have led to any untoward incident but now she feels that she was in someone's protection, someone who was showering upon her the colors of life.

As for love, Rabies's heart bells seldom rang. There was an urge to be loved in her teenage years, but it never materialized. She was the sole sister of eight brothers. Her family provided an over-protective environment. She was free to move around but only with family members. She was under a dense shadow of love. But at times the shadow of taller trees stops the growth of tiny plants underneath. Her mother was a strict disciplinarian. In her childhood Rabia visited many places but only in her dreams. But she loved that. Small incidents were enough to make her happy.

Uncle Zaheer is a sophisticated person. Our meeting in a conference was an impromptu one. Rabia felt a positive energy radiating from Uncle. Subsequent meetings and candid discussions turned her feelings of positivity into a firm impression about him. He too shared his personal experiences with Rabia. Rabia told him all about her creative works. In those days Rabia was entangled with a literary group who were all set to publish the compilation without her consent. Rabia was upset at losing her seven years' hard-earned work. She had made the mistake of trusting those people and handing them her compilation without an agreement. She shared her agony with Uncle Zaheer. His response was: "I already told you not to work with those people. Anyway, if tension intensifies, do come to me. When people who share their worries with me, I usually get rid of them." It happened exactly he had said. Rabia never knew who helped and how? Rabia's honor was saved by the Divine Power called Allah. Rabia offered two *Nafal* [special prayer] and requested Allah to help, like he sent Divine help to the Muslim Army in the *"Battle of Badr"* in the early days of Islam. Rabia then did some charity work, and gave alms; then she dispatched her original compilation to another publisher, National Book Foundation – Islamabad. The people who had stolen her work were astonished and were not sure that original work would ever be published with her name. They sent Rabia harassing messages. Mental worry leads to panic attacks. She went into a semi-conscious state. When she was well again, people were telling her: "It is hard to live in Rome and fight with the Pope. You are a woman, a weak creature of society having no reference, connection, high status or wealth. You should surrender." Rabia replied that with silence. After few months, Rabia received a call around midnight from Amna Mufti "Congratulations! Your book, *Urdu Afsana Ehd e Hazer Mein* has been published by the National Book Foundation – Islamabad". Rabia could not believe her ears. All worldly powers; wealth, materialism, friendships and public relations had lost the battle. The divine Power had won.

Over the last twelve years, Rabia feels that there is an invisible power that always helps her. Whenever Rabia is in trouble, she seeks divine help through Sadqa [alms]. It works, she is sure. If even for some reason it does not work sometimes, she still has peace of mind.

Dervish has asked a strange question regarding her creativity. Rabia is afraid to answer. She is afraid of narcissism, pride and boasting. Rabia just wants to say that secrets should remain secrets. Only that part of a secret should be revealed that might guide another person. A secret must remain a secret till the end. The beauty of a secret lies in its keeping.

O Dervish! "A secret within a secret" takes her leave.

Good Morning.

Twenty-Second Dream

Spirituality, Psychology and Esoteric Experience

27th May 2018

Salam to Eastern Rabia from a Western Dervish!

Dervish earnestly wishes to tell Rabia that although he did not start a traditional family he did create a family of his friends. He calls them 'Family of the Heart'. 'Family of the Heart' constitutes his likeminded friends. He will introduce to Rabia the men and women of this family in absentia. They are the friends with whom Dervish passes his evenings. They inspire him to think and write.

On reading Rabia's letter Dervish went into a solace for a while. He then read the letter again to absorb the hidden meanings and complexity. Dervish considers himself lucky that Rabia trusts him so much that she gave him access to her innermost secrets. Dervish has no hesitation in accepting the truth that his interest is limited to the psychology of spirituality. It seems to him that in the company of mystics, Rabia has traversed quite a distance towards her truth. She also seems to have had a few esoteric experiences. Dervish is quite aware of the fact that there are numerous mysteries around him.

Life is a mystery; death is a mystery.

Poetry a mystery and awareness too is a mystery.

Since Dervish is a student of science and psychology, therefore he attaches these mysteries to the laws of nature and not to God or religion. He is well-conversant with the fact that science, medicine and psychology have progressed very fast in last few centuries. It has resolved many mysteries. The secrets of ancient times are no longer secrets today. He firmly hopes that in upcoming decades scientists will unveil more secrets and humans will understand better the universe around them. Arif wrote a verse about this phenomenon:

During the journey to know myself,

I acquired a whole world of knowledge.

When Dervish was a university student, it was surprising for him to learn that in the old religious era of West, the word "Psyche" meant "Soul." Now in this secular era in the West, "Psyche'" means "Mind".

When Dervish ponders about the seven billion people around him, he finds them attached to various traditions. Four billion are followers of organized religions, two billion have a spiritual tradition, while the remaining one billion people adhere to the secular and scientific tradition. Since Dervish adheres to the secular and scientific tradition, he does not believe in God, religion, soul, heaven or hell. Dervish feels that his and Rabia's friendship is that of a believer and a non-believer. But the most beautiful side of this friendship is that both respect each other's person and respective philosophy of life. In today's era of extremism, this phenomenon is hard to, if not impossible. Dervish surmises that in this world, there are as many truths as the humans themselves. Every human holds fast, respects and protects his own truth. While penning this letter, Dervish feels that he has shared his philosophical truth with Rabia as she had shared her spiritual truth with him. Dervish's difference of opinion with Rabia is in fact a manifestation of his trust in her.

In one of her previous letters Rabia had written a few sentences about some Pharaoh of knowledge. She wanted to share but was tired and had to postpone it. Similarly, she had also deferred the mention of man-woman relationships. Dervish is softly reminding her, lest she forgets, as she writes at night using her conscious and subconscious minds.

Dervish must interview one of his philosopher friends Abrar ul Hassan, on history. He therefore requests to take leave of Rabia.

Twenty-Third Dream

Women, Islam and Divorce

29th May 2018

An after-midnight greeting to Dervish!

O Dervish! Rabia is not focused these days due to her ailment. Please forgive her for being so scattered while writing. Rabia at this moment hears the blowing of Ramadhan sirens. This is done to wake Muslims for the next fasting. They eat their morning meals before dawn to fast from dawn to dusk. In cities, people remain awake through the night and sleep after taking their morning meals. But the blowing of sirens is a tradition. In society like ours, the traditions must be kept alive at all costs.

O Dervish! Rabia has been a student of life, the life that is a mix of enlightenment and ignorance. Rabia feels that one day scientific research will prove the existence of God. On that day everything shall cease to exist. Then a new life will emerge from a new beginning.

Rabia agrees with the idea: "This universe holds as many truths as there are humans – their stories, questions, hypotheses and outcomes." If a person could fully understand this phenomenon he or she could live a peaceful life. This life is an intricate riddle. To understand all facets human life is too short.

O Dervish! Rabia has been gloomy since yesterday. She feels as if she has just parted with her daughter. Rabia has grown a garden of love like flowers. She looks after these flowers of unconditional love all the time. She does not consider it necessary to meet those, whom she loves. She is not a free bird like Dervish. Despite her earnest desire, Rabia cannot fly in free space. Therefore, she keeps cherishing the love of her garden without meeting or talking. One of these flowers is the love of her elder aunt Shahnaz, who was staying with her for a few weeks. Her departure has made her sad. But she must adhere to a saying that people who have homes must return to their homes.

Since yesterday Rabia is recalling Dervish's words; inspire and intimidate. She is thinking that the process of getting inspired is tarnished by the intimidation. Inspiration is a positive attribute whereas intimidation a negative one. It is done to cover one's own weak personality. Idol worship does not bear fruit. Thus, it should be done away with.

Rabia remembers her questions pertaining to man and woman friendship. Rabia feels that Man is action and Woman just a reaction. All actions are initiated by man, the woman just responds to his actions. This ratio is Five to Ninety-Five. If man shows a 5% love towards woman, she reciprocates with 95% love. Similarly, if man shows 5% indifference he in turn should be ready to receive 95% coldness from his counterpart. This formula is visible in every walk of life and in every man-woman relationship. The only condition is that life should be seen with open eyes. This Action – Reaction does not need spoken words. This is an invisible chemistry that works even it is found deep in the hearts or minds of the people. The Reaction starts unknowingly. It is a scientific phenomenon. Rabia believes that one day science will prove the authenticity of spiritualism. Rabia's own life experience tells her the same. Every man-woman relationship revolves around the action-reaction process. It is due to the physiology of woman that her reaction is always belated and severe.

Rabia understood the woman's love through the law of divorce prevalent in Islam. A woman's psyche is extreme in nature. If she does not wish to live with someone, no power on earth can force her to do so. Wealth and power have no leverage to deal with a woman. If she wishes to drop a name it is forever, no compromise. However the male psyche is quite different. He can get back to the woman he broke with earlier.

If we talk of Urdu literature, Rabia is of the view that men's real character has not been portrayed by male writers. They could not write a man's character even themselves. A man has a different psyche altogether. He has not written anything about himself. It seems as if he has been writing to impress women. He has been portraying an imaginary woman in his writings or fabricating his own character to understand women. Man writer wrote many characters of women. He also received appreciation from critics as well. But alas! It was his own truth about women, not necessarily the women themselves. In fact, the true picture of woman emerged when woman started writing herself. Male writers could not comprehensibly write about true male characters. He just made sketches.

You pick up the list of university level literary thesis, you would find similar topics like: "The feminist aspects contained in so and so fiction…"

No pertinent findings or conclusions have been given by the writers in those theses. It shows that degrees do not change the behaviors and mindsets. The more men educate themselves, more oppressive they become towards women. Men carry out an organized physical, mental, oral and emotional exploitation of women through all possible means. They do it each and every time without knowing that the process of Karma has commenced around them – "What goes around comes around." Rabia is aggrieved to say that she lives in a society where degrees are obtained in abundance, yet no increase in knowledge. Society is practically taking a downward flight. Here nobody wants to take an upward flight, save a few people whose life has been made miserable by their materialistic environment. They are either killed or go insane. There are many clouts of knowledge Pharaohs around Rabia. They always move in groups. At times she feels pity for them.

Over here Rabia has witnessed many knowledgeable Abu Jehals [Father of Ignorance]. Rabia believes in Nature that is the reason she became friend with a non-believer. Rabia respects freedom of expression, freedom of living and human respect. That is enough to live a peaceful life.

Rabia requests leave from Dervish as two spans of time (day/night) are meeting over here. Rabia respects their union. She keenly prays for their pleasant mating. She is quite aware of the agony of the void within.

Goodbye to a Wandering Dervish.

Twenty-Fourth Dream

Poetry in Prose

30th May 2018

Dervish says Salam to Rabia - the night vigilant!

Rabia's letter was not only disoriented but also complicated and serious. Dervish found it hard to dig out its essence without repeated readings. Dervish also felt as if Rabia wrote a poetry in prose that contains flash of wisdom. When Dervish was reading her dream a couplet was revealed to him:

'When Rabia is in an ecstatic trance

The words are doing a whirling dance'

When Rabia translates her thoughts, experiences and ideas into words, the words feel too small to convey the feelings. Then Dervish struggles to find concealed meanings in her words. Dervish wishes not only to know what Rabia writes or thinks but what she wishes to think and write. At times Rabia's letters appear like an Afsana [short story], at others an abstract story as the creativity overtakes the message. This is a higher stage of creativity, where the messages can only be felt, they cannot be translated. Dervish feels as if Rabia is slowly revealing herself to him.

Rabia has quizzed Dervish about the secrets of human relations. Well! Being a student of human psychology Dervish has studied numerous theories proffered by various psychologists. He would like to share two theorists. The first is Sigmund Freud. He opines that human beings are fundamentally pleasure-seekers. Their entire life revolves around searching for happiness and pleasure. The second is Harry Stack Sullivan who professed that human beings need something more than just happiness or pleasure. They do have a need for companionship, friendly relations, and emotional support. At times marriages do so well, hurting the couples; but they do not want to separate because they don't want to be left alone. They think that a bad relationship is better than no relationship at all. Sullivan's theory suggests that loneliness is the greatest emotional suffering for a human. There are very few people who can live happily in solitude.

While reading Rabia's last letter, Dervish came across Rabia's remarks about oppressors, self-projectionists and opportunists. Rabia called them 'Literary Pharaohs' and 'Fathers of Ignorance'. Dervish then recalled some writers, poets and scholars who suffer from narcissism. Dervish had once written a humorous essay about such characters. Its title was "Peace be upon me". Rabia has a grievance against male story writers who have not been able to fully comprehend male psychology never mind albeit the female. Dervish is of the view that to understand oneself and then express it in a creative manner is an uphill task. Not everyone can do it. The writers mentioned by Rabia live in the East where religion and tradition have produced a suffocating environment. No creativity can take place in an atmosphere of suppression. Dervish once wrote:

"The walls of traditions were built so tall and strong

For generations, no one could see out and beyond"

The Urdu story writer has not yet become intellectually free; he cannot capture the complete picture of a man. He is handicapped by a preoccupation with women as object of lust. She has not yet become his friend. On this Dervish has a short poem:

"Forgetting about physical pleasure

For a while, let us talk to each other"

Eastern men and women have not yet learned to communicate, regardless of gender. Despite all these issues, Dervish is optimistic that humans are traversing a steady journey of evolution. He seeks to unveil the mysteries of life. Dervish's first poetry collection was named *Talash* [The Search]. His search continues even today. Dervish thinks himself lucky that in this search, he has found a few sincere, sensitive and understanding men and women with whom he can open his heart. He is happy that he came across Rabia through the Internet. From thousands of miles away he can have a literary dialogue with her.

Dervish would like to inquire of Rabia, what is her idea of a successful writer? Does she consider herself a successful writer?

Dervish requests to take his leave of Rabia. He must rush to his clinic where his patients are waiting for him.

Twenty-Fifth Dream

A Woman Who Lives in Two Worlds

30th May 2018

O Dervish! A fatigued night presents its greetings.

A strange phenomenon has overwhelmed Rabia. Her mind often flies to another world. This happens unconsciously, she does not know the destination of her flights. She forgets what she wrote at night. Her own script looks strange to her the next morning. Since her childhood she has been travelling in two worlds. People surrounding her think that she is groggy. Family members have concluded that Rabia is not mentally with them most of the time. This feeling is more intense when Rabia is alone. In seclusion, she lives in her own world. She is writing about her mental state because there may be some writing done by Rabia from the other world. Dervish is requested to feel free to seek clarification from Rabia about what she wrote in any previous letter.

As for writers, Rabia is of the view that you cannot become a writer if you do not have certain genes in you. However, a weak writer may become a strong writer through sheer practice. Rabia once asked Uncle Irfan: "I wanted to become an artist or lecturer. Why did I become a writer?" Uncle replied: "Only the Creator knows the exact number of doctors, engineers, teachers and philosophers needed by the world. Had the system of the universe rested with humans, they would have wrecked it. The Pen has great value as the Creator has sworn upon the pen in the Holy Quran. The Holy Book also urges humans to ponder the Universe again and again."

Rabia does not describe herself as "writer" even though she is a published writer. To put it in simple words, to make her solitude meaningful, she started to write. The pastime made her life colorful. Rabia writes for her catharsis. When she is not writing anything, she turns peevish. During this period, she is so frustrated that she picks fights over trivial issues. She therefore avoids arguments with family members to forestall such incidents.

While compiling *Urdu Afsana Ehde Hazir Mein*, Rabia had an opportunity to meet and interview four hundred writers. She has named it "Global Urdu Pen-Land." It was a beautiful experience. It included meetings with successful, average and below-average writers. Rabia has also described it in the preface of her compilation. If she must describe them in metaphors, she would call them; flowers, thorns, clay and water. Perhaps the galaxy of writers is composed of such chemistry. She received a lot of love, beauty, attitudes, pains, stories, relationships and sincerity. Rabia found shallow people in the tall personalities and great humans in apparently small ones. In short the world with all its colors shown to Rabia.

After that, Rabia has viewed success and failure from a different angle. Rabia concluded that those people who came across as renowned writers were also great men, in stature, manners and character. The great fiction works were created by great men. A tiny man can only produce a trivial work. The latter come on social media and say: "In fact our stories are abstract and symbolic, these cannot be understood by ordinary people." This question is as complicated as life itself. There are no fixed formulas to resolve the riddle. In this context, Rabia would like to share some interesting happenings that took place while interacting with Ahmed Nadeem Qasmi, Amjad Islam Amjad, Mansoora Ahmed, Muntansar Husain Tarar, Musharaf Alam Zouqi, Gulzar Sahib, Syed Muhammad Ashraf, Israr Gandhi and Ashfaq Ahmed. But not now. Currently, she needs some rest. Rabia now wants to move from here. She wants to live in some far away land, where life does not present such challenges. She wants to live some part of her life for herself. For now, she is living this life for others in compliance with the prevailing traditions and customs. Her well-wishers and sincere friends appreciate her for such noble deeds. But she is not doing it for that. She heeds neither virtue nor sin. Rabia just wants to breathe peacefully in seclusion and solitude, breathing in the fresh air. Does Dervish have any such similar desire?

With this question, Rabia says goodnight to Dervish.

Twenty-Sixth Dream

A Long-Held Dream

31st May 2018

Dervish's Salam to an exhausted Rabia!

Dervish is recalling Buddha's quote: "The covered distance should not be measured by miles, but by the fatigue caused to the traveler."

Gradually, Dervish is realizing that Rabia reads his letters around midnight, then answers in a subconscious state of mind. Dervish is lucky that he receives Rabia's true and pure thoughts with no tinge of artificiality, formality or showing off. Rabia's words flow from the spring of her heart and spread onto the paper. Dervish had some reservations about the continuity of Rabia's letters in view of her increased domestic chores during the month of Ramadan. He has been surprised that the letters have been pouring in until today, the last day of May. Dervish is also pleasantly surprised that he and Rabia together wrote over a hundred pages and more than twenty thousand words within a month. The creative juice is flowing like a river. Continuously writing literary letters for a month is a no less than a literary miracle.

Dervish often muses about creativity, which holds pains and pleasures for the writer. Dervish had experienced ecstasy when he wrote his autobiography within a month. In that, he continuously wrote twenty thousand words to complete the book called *The Seeker*. The book was in English and Dervish had written it all by himself.

Writing creative letters with the help of an intellectual woman was Dervish's long held dream. Dervish is thankful to Rabia for turning this dream into reality. The pain and pleasure of this discourse is mutual.

While, Dervish is not only obtaining satisfaction from this but also experiencing a creative euphoria. He is also fully aware that the act of creativity has connected labor-pains. In the words of Arif:

A blissful mental agony is at its peak

Verse is created when a poet's brain reek

Dervish is happy that Rabia seeks pleasure from writing. Like some people acquire happiness by producing children, writers achieve bliss by giving birth to their books. Dervish knows that Rabia was student of literature at the University. Dervish has been a student of psychology. In past years, he has not only interviewed numerous poets and writers but has read biographies of many philosophers and scholars. He has also treated many mentally sick artists in his clinic. After years of observation, experience and study, Dervish has devised a theory about the human personality. He uses this theory in his clinic. Dervish wishes to share few parts of his theory with Rabia so that she understands his thesis. Dervish may be pardoned for using English words as the theory was originally written in English. Dervish opines that "Every child is born with a natural personality. Dervish calls it the 'Natural Self.' In the first few years the Natural Self divides itself into two parts. The first part is the 'Conditioned Self', which is evolved under the influence of family, religion and culture. This part tells the child 'What he/she should do.' On the other hand, the second part is the manifestation of the Creative Self.' This part tells the person; 'What he/she loves to do.'

In traditional people, who are in the majority, the "Conditioned Self" is greater than the "Creative Self", whereas in poets, writers, artists and scholars who are in the minority, the "Creative Self" overwhelms the "Conditioned Self." Dervish's takes into account the genes as well, because poets, writers and artist tend to have other artists in their families. When poets, writers and artists realize that there is an artist sleeping within them, they either ignore him or wake him. Dervish was lucky in this regard. He not only looked after the writer in him but also groomed him. Therefore, he was able to create many books.

When Dervish used to live in the East he followed the path of 20% "love to do" and 80% "should do." On moving to the West, he created a new life for himself. That gave him creative freedom. Now Dervish lives a life of 80% "love to do" and 20% "should do." He is now happy with his life. He can freely write whatever he thinks. Therefore, he considers himself a fortunate and successful writer. Other than this, being a therapist, he advises 10-12 patients on daily basis as to how can they turn their agonies into happiness. This is how he serves humanity.

Dervish once wrote about his creations, "My creations are my love letters to humanity." Dervish hopes this has reduced Rabia's fatigue. She will now tell him about the interesting events involving Ahmed Nadeem Qasmi and Amjad Islam Amjad whom Dervish has also met. He too has a few anecdotes that he would like to share with Rabia.

Now Dervish shall wait for another midnight letter from Rabia.

Goodnight.

Twenty-Seventh Dream

Life is Slipping out of Hands Like Sand…

31st May 2018

O Dervish! Accept the midnight greetings!

Rabia's heart and mind both suffer from an agony of parting with creativity. No human around her is aware of her agony and painful state of mood. Rabia is in a low mood nowadays. Like her creative friend Dervish, Rabia too wishes to move away from here. She wishes to fly the skies and seven seas, to never return. She desires to spend some time with herself, live for herself, fly for herself and smile for herself. Rabia has everything that most women wish for but does not have what she wishes for herself. For few years, she has wanted to live with her dreams and desires. Rabia wants to sleep and wake up when she wishes. She dreams of sitting by the lake or on river banks, reading books all day long. She also wises to watch a movie then enjoy thinking about it with a cup of coffee, sitting in a balcony or window of a lonely house, all by herself.

At this moment, Rabia feels fed up with the majority traditional segment of society. She thinks of herself as not only a misfit, but also unwanted. The home, family and social environment are far from her mindset. In such a mental state Dervish's letters are acting as Rabia's lifeline. When in a low, writing letters takes her on a mental flight, the flight that cruises high in the sky and beyond the moon. The invisible and apparently meaningless imaginations are now reasons to live. Either she would have been passing her last days in a mental hospital or be buried under tons of soil. She lived a very hard and stressed life. As the life was saying good-bye to her, a ray of hope emerged out of nowhere. It emerged towards the end of her life. Rabia has not yet understood life and its ups and downs.

Rabia wishes to ask Dervish the definition of a "Successful Writer." Not only Dervish but also Rabia enjoys the peaceful bliss of a creative journey together. She considers herself lucky to be a co-traveler with a man who has ideas and theories. He is not a follower. He does not go with the flow, he is rather himself a flow. He is not an opportunist, nor is he over whelmed by lust. He is a humanist, thus very composed. This has brought Rabia closer to him and this quality in a man is in fact known as manhood. On the contrary, an ordinary man is hard to control. He is full of unnatural urge and barbarianism. An ordinary woman, mother or beloved provokes in a common man the desire to receive the material gains. But a sophisticated and well-groomed woman would never tolerate such nonsense. She would rather avoid him. In retaliation the man considering it a disgrace, endeavors to take revenge and win over her.

Rabia is grateful that Dervish is a real man. Had he not been so humane, Rabia could never have continued the journey of this beautiful discourse. That is why she was apprehensive about the continuity of the letters until the twelfth one. In the past whenever she worked with an Asian male partner the journey never achieved success. Then she decided to do her creative work alone. Thus she locked the door of her heart to any co-traveler.

O Dervish! To narrate the interesting anecdotes about the writers who met Rabia during her compilations she needs a certain focus. That is not available to her for now. A hurried discourse can tarnish the beauty of it. So, she is postponing.

Rabia may not be a beauty-lover but she certainly is a beauty admirer. Rabia is also impressed by outer beauty. She feels that apparent beauty is in fact the manifestation of inner beauty. What does enriched and experienced Dervish have to say about it? Does the outer beauty of a person reveal his or her inner beauty or vice versa? Rabia has been pondering over it a long time.

Rabia too has been aspiring for some time to have a creative dialogue like this one but it was not possible with a person of the opposite gender. Rabia lives in a society where all creativity, research, informative science and psychological discourses end up with the man-woman mentality. Whether a woman agrees or not the man's instinct is to make a sexual advance towards her. When lust takes over a creative friendship, all knowledge, intellect and theories discharge like semen. The semen that is not strong enough to produce life in a woman's womb. When a character is weak, then focus would be diminished and ultimately lost.

Dervish and Rabia are fortunate to have acquired a higher level of consciousness. A level where seeking knowledge from each other is a blissful experience. The creative juice is flowing without any hindrance. Both are committed to their creative work. This twenty-seventh letter is proof of their sincere commitment to their cause.

O Dervish! Solitude has prevailed throughout this serene night. Rabia is just listening to her breathing. The air is still as though it were waiting for a departed beloved. It seems as though this new day will be a hotter one. It will be the first day of the new month. But the old life will have taken another leap forward.

Today Rabia feels like life is slipping from her hands like grains of sand. Now only a few grains are left. She cannot hold them any longer. They will also soon slip away, all the dreams dwelling in her eyes and her heart full of love will be buried with her in the grave.

Life is a mystery. This mystery has never been revealed to anyone in the past nor is there any chance of a revelation in the future. Her mysterious self needs to sleep. Rabia had a sleepless night yesterday. Perhaps another life within her was restless.

A bell rings in seventh layer of the heavens.

Good night and Good morning to a seven-seas-apart Dervish.

Twenty-Eighth Dream

Wealth, Fame and Woman

1ˢᵗ June 2018

Dervish says Adaab to Night-Vigilant Rabia!

Dervish is impressed by Rabia's sincerity and her regard for creative moments. He is recalling Mirza Ghalib's line:

Love demands patience, but the desire is over whelming…

Dervish is fully aware of Rabia's misery. He knows that when a member of the creative minority, a poet, writer, play wright or artist is born in a traditional family, what torment he or she has to endure. The agony becomes more intense if the artist is a woman. The traditional people want to control her future, her art and her life on the pretext of guarding her character and honor. How many women become victims of such oppression and surrender, is anybody's guess. Dervish is impressed by Rabia because her physical self may be confined within a "traditional ambience", but her mind is free. Her outer self may be suppressed but her inner self is like a free bird who keeps flying in the free space of thoughts. The world of imagination and thoughts is infinite. Dervish would like to quote Ghalib once again:

Hay KahaN Tamanna ka Doosra Qadam Ya Rab

Ham nay Dasht-eImkanK Ko Aik Naqsh-e-Pa, Paya

O Lord! Where is the second step of human curiosity?

A single footprint contains in it the enormous possibility

Dervish, being a psychotherapist is also fully aware that artists who cannot keep their "free bird" alive in the stringent atmosphere of tradition either suffer from a psychological trauma or commit suicide.

While reading biographies, Dervish came across Meer Taqi Meer's. He had suffered mental trauma in his youth. In the words of Ali Sardar Jafri: "For many months Meer chose to remain secluded in his home". He would not go out. Whenever he went out, the youngsters who considered him insane would throw pebbles at him. He perceived a woman on the surface of the moon and he has written a lot about her in his poetry. After a few months, he came out of that mental state. But the influence of the crisis stayed with him for a long time, and throughout his life. Meer remained taciturn. People considered him arrogant, but he was in a psychological trance. Dervish has written a comprehensive essay; "Meer's Poetry and Insanity." It became quite controversial. Other than Meer, Dervish also read about Jaun Elia who suffered from depression. On the other hand, Munir Niazi drank his suffering through wine. Munir Niazi wrote:

I was better than other, was my shortcoming,

I was never equal to anyone in my surrounding

These were the stories of Eastern artists. If one looks at few Western artists; Virginia Wolf, Sylvia Plinth, Earnest Hemmingway and Vincent Van Gogh committed suicide. At times, for some artists living becomes harder than dying. German philosopher Schopenhauer once said: "When the horrors of living outweigh the horrors of dying, people commit suicide."

When Dervish read about great artists, he concluded that there is an intimate relation between creativity and insanity. He therefore named his clinic "Creative Psychotherapy Clinic." There he provides therapy to many artists, writers and poets. There people have more severe psychological issues than traditional people. These issues are hindrances to become a successful artist. The traditional psychiatrist treats these creative people through medication. They do not know that their peace of mind is connected to their creative work.

Rabia has asked Dervish, what make a successful writer. Well in Dervish's view, the successful writer is the one who knows how to creatively express his truth. The one who knows his medium and the message contained in the medium. The one who knows what he has to offer to humanity. The successful writer remains immersed in his work, without bothering what others think about him. Ghalib says:

I least expect others to admire my verse nor do I expect a pat

If people think my poetry has no message, let it be like that

Since Dervish is a male, he knows the challenges of being a male writer. These are; Wealth, Fame and Woman. The writer who can successfully deal with these three tests can work with full concentration, remaining committed to his Muse. The Muse considers wealth, fame and women her rivals and opponents. The successful writer knows that: "The creative journey is a marathon, not a hundred-meter sprint." Due to this Dervish likes turtles. If Rabia ever visited Dervish's clinic she would see hundreds of them. The process of therapy is as slow as the creative self-awareness journey to one's self.

O the night-vigilant Rabia! Every male artist conceals a Dervish within him, and every female artist, a Rabia who reveals itself at an appropriate time. Then slowly its creativity and personality reveals itself to the entire world.

Dervish and Rabia are neither just two names, nor just two humans, rather they are two symbols, two metaphors, two banks of the river of life connected through the bridge of creativity. They are also two co-travelers who have embarked upon the journey to seek themselves and the truth of the universe. The truth that is being revealed unto humanity through poets, writers, artists, saints, mystics, philosophers and scholars. The seekers of truth belong to one family, one caravan and one clan. Each member of this tribe emits the fragrance of sincerity, compassion and love for humanity. It is so unfortunate that individuals of this minority family must pay a price for their freedom. At times the price is too high. The traditional majority either exiles them, imprison them or hangs them. In the words of Baksh Lyallpury:

Though we live in a small city here

But we own a large slaughter-house over here

Dervish wished to write more to answer another of her questions, but he went into the ecstasy of a conscious and sub conscious trance. Now his slumber and dreams are calling him. He requests leave from Rabia. Whenever Dervish puts his head on his pillow to sleep slumber lovingly takes him into her arms and lulls him to sleep.

Twenty-Ninth Dream

A Mysterious Dream

1st June 2018

Rabia says hello and hi to Dervish!

From this faraway land without saying a word, travelling over the airwaves, I am sure my greeting will reach Dervish at the speed of light.

Rabia liked Dervish's experience of going to sleep immediately when the slumber takes him into a loving lap. Rabia has been yearning to enjoy such a slumber for so long. In the words of Uncle Ghalib:

HazaruN KhawaisheN Aisi kay Har Khwawaish Pe Damm Niklay

Everyone here yearns to fulfill his thousand wishes and each one is breathtaking…

Irfan ul Haq says: "One who reads books becomes knowledgeable and the one who reads people becomes a Dervish. Rabia feels happy that Dervish is a psychiatrist, who treats ailing people. Rabia was amused by the theory proffered by Dervish that says: "Wealth, Fame and Woman are considered rivals by the "Muse." It may surprise Dervish that in Rabia's society, wealth, fame and woman are the first choice of men. He considers them the rivals of the Muse. The Creative Muse is the rival of men over here.

Rabia agrees with Dervish that many women artist abandon their passion under the pressure of the Traditional Majority. Some men also surrender. She is not sure but she thinks that these artists (men and women) are co-travelers of pain and permanent suffering. Their union creates an encouragement for each other. In the words of

Rabia Basri: "Without the will of Nature no one can regret and return." Those who buckle under the pressure of the 'Traditional Majority' were not given perseverance and patience. They are weak from the inside. The external pressure is just a nail in their coffin. Rabia too thought many times that she must quit writing, she could not be an artist. She wanted to call it a day. But circumstances brought her back to the journey of creativity. Then she realized that there is some invisible power who kept her composed so that she could follow her heart. Humans are puppets on invisible strings.

When Rabia was a small girl, her Baba taught her to walk at night. He used to take her along to the literary gatherings of Lahore on moonlit nights. In those gatherings numerous serious artists used to talk about film, TV, Radio, literature and paintings. Rabia could not understand the discussions but enjoyed that a lot. She was the only child present amongst the elders. The surprises in her life started at that small age. In this way, she had met many renowned writers of their times at the age of three or four. At that time, she had not thought of becoming a writer.

Then she enrolled in Government College Lahore. She had never thought of becoming a Ravian. After her graduation, Rabia entered the University of Punjab. However, she felt like a "misfit" there. She felt burdened, but consoled herself with the argument that it was just a matter of two years. Then one day something happened that forced her to think that humans are puppets controlled by a Divine Power.

At that time, she met Sohail Ahmed Khan – Head of the Urdu Department. Rabia was introduced to Mr. Sohail by one of her friends. He said: "How did our student join Government College?" Rabia considered it a compliment. Then there was some issue with her degree that took some time to be corrected. Rabia got frustrated and left the University of Punjab. She had decided to say good bye to formal education. Meanwhile as luck would have it, Rabia had an opportunity to visit an exhibition in the Alhamra Art Gallery. An artist had done an awesome calligraphy on Surah-e-Yousef. Impressed by the artist's work, Rabia went to meet him. The discussion with the artist came around to her admission issue. He advised Rabia to visit Ghazi Ilam Deen Shaheed's shrine, pray there, and beg for the fixing of her admission problem. Hopefully, she would benefit from going there. Lovers never return from the beloved without a gift. Rabia was not sure about it. However, on one hot summer noon Rabia went to his shrine. She does not remember what she prayed over there as she was more mesmerized by the ambience of Miami Sahib Graveyard.

Even today the place haunts Rabia as it is full of mysterious solitude. At night while sleeping she dreamed that she was climbing a slope, surrounded by green plants and it was raining. She could not recognize the place. A year later when she went to appear in the GC University Entry Test, she climbed the same slope among the green trees, and it was raining. Rabia recalled her dream. Now she thinks that it was a simple affair. Why were there so many twists in the story?

On the day of her interview Rabia was not feeling well. She requested the girl ahead of her to let her go before her. She agreed to the request. The girl was no other than Hina Mohsin, who became good friends with Rabia.

There were three faculty members in the Interview Room, namely Dr. Saadat Saeed, Dr. Tariq Zaidi and another member. One of the members asked Rabia: "Why you say *Raja Gidh* is your favorite book? Why not Holy Quran?" Rabia replied: "Sir you did not ask about a Divine book." The other member asked, "While answering the question about your favorite poem, you wrote Iqbal's poem, why not a romantic poem by any other poet, say;

Ghalib?" Rabia answered: "You asked my favorite poem, so I wrote the one:

Raise your self-esteem to such a height

That God before writing every fate

Should ask a soul what it wills

"Self" is the only attribute most people fail to protect and raise. In this way, Rabia became a Ravian. Now some talk about literature and writing. Rabia was chosen as Co-Editor of the College Magazine *Ravi*. She worked there for one year until she was forcefully asked to quit. As Co-Editor Rabia has many good memories. Once, she requested Ahmed Nadeem Qasmi to send his poetry for *Ravi*. Seven days passed but she did not receive a letter with his poetry. Rabia called Qasmi Sahib only to hear his labored breathing as if he was not well. When Rabia politely introduced herself, he said he remembered her and that he had dispatched his poetry that on very day. But Qasmi Sahib was finding it hard to speak. He was being transported to the hospital. That was her last conversation with him. The next day he passed away. The purpose of telling the story is that despite being on his death bed he remembered the promise made to a student. He was such a great man. He never ignored his manners even in anger and pain.

Now Rabia wants to narrate an anecdote about Amjad Islam Amjad. Once Rabia went to his office to collect a CD. She was pleasantly surprised to see Anwar Masood sitting in his office. Anwar Sahib asked Rabia whether she writes verse. Rabia reluctantly showed a few pages of poetry to both poets. Having seen that, Amjad Sahib advised Rabia to write prose and said that he would guide her and groom her as writer. Amjad Sahib kept his words without making a lame excuse even once. Rabia then realized that a great writer is in fact a great man, a man of character. Character decides destiny, a great writer must have a sound character; without that he or she is shallow.

O Dervish! It's time to say hello and hi to the One who resides in heavens. The night-vigilant Rabia wishes to have a word with him. After a while there will be milky light all around, and the burning sun will rise. There are so many topics to discuss but Rabia begs to take her leave with one last question; "What is the relationship between humbleness and greatness?"

Stay in the protection of God, O Dervish.

Thirtieth Dream

Family of the Heart

2nd June 2018

Dervish presents Salam to Rabia's human-friendly nature.

Reading about Ahmed Nadeem Qasmi in Rabia's last letter, Dervish also recalled his two meetings with him. He first met Ahmed Nadeem Qasmi in Peshawar. Those were the days when Dervish was a student of medicine at Khyber Medical College. A few friends had organized a poetry recital, but they could muster only Two Thousand rupees to meet the expenses. Dervish was astonished to learn that the renowned poets of Pakistan were segmented into three groups. The first group that included Ahmed Faraz, charged PKR (Pakistani Rupees) 1000 to recite his poetry. The second group that included Ahmed Nadeem Qasmi who could be hired for PKR 500 The third group charged PKR 200 to read their poetry in any function. The third group included poets like Mohsin Ehsan, Khatir Ghaznvi and Farigh Bokhari.

In those days Ahmed Faraz was Director of the Peshawar Arts Council. Dervish, along with organizers of the event, went to see him in his office. They told him, "Sir we wish to invite you for a poetry symposium but unfortunately we do not have PKR 1000." Ahmed Faraz smiled and replied, "Don't worry, I will come." He did come as promised and recited his poetry. Dervish still remembers one of his verses:

"Then, it so happened that we found solace with outsiders

Hateful treatment by own people sent us to the outsiders"

At culmination of recital when Dervish asked Ahmed Faraz the thought behind the verse, he replied,

"The creation of Bangladesh from East Pakistan with the help of India."

When Dervish read the account of Rabia's conversation with Ahmed Nadeem Qasmi, he recalled Qasmi's verse:

I won't die, when death comes around me

I am like a river, would dive into the sea.

Dervish's second meeting with Qasmi Sahib was in Toronto. It was a special occasion. The poets and writers of Toronto had organized a seminar to celebrate the 75th birthday of Qasmi. Dervish cherishes the memory of reading an essay in the seminar: the 'Relationship of God and Humans in Qasmi's Poetry.' After his talk at the seminar, Qasmi Sahib remarked, "Many articles have been written about my poetry, but this essay was unique and different..." His comments made Dervish's day. These words were so complimentary that Dervish felt well rewarded for his hard work.

Ahmed Faraz was once interviewed by Dervish in a seminar in Canada. The hall was packed. To a question by Dervish as to why he had not written his autobiography, Faraz replied, "I do not want to write a half-truth and my people are not yet prepared to learn my whole truth." Dervish knows that poets, writers and scholars are part of the Creative Minority. They are often oppressed by the Traditional Majority. With this in mind, Dervish with the help of his friends has made a forum in Canada, which he calls: "Family of the Heart." This group regularly organizes literary, social and philosophical programs. Its aim is to encourage amateur writers. New writers should learn from veterans the secrets of writing as well as the secrets of life. In this context, Dervish rejoiced his meeting with a writer and scholar from London. Naseer Habib was brought to Whitby from Toronto by Rasheed Nadeem who is an active member of the Family of the Heart as well as a close friend of Dervish. Dervish adores Nadeem and often recites his verse:

My city has no forbearance anymore

So I do not wish to live here anymore

After the program, Naseer Habib expressed his emotions, thoughts and impressions about the Family of the Heart. Dervish felt very happy to hear him speak excellent Urdu. He had never heard such fluent Urdu. Dervish would like to share his impressions with Rabia so that she gets an idea about what people think about the above described forum:

"To the people of the heart ..... Self – conceit held in the outer beauty makes one embark upon the journey to the newer places. Yet there is another journey. The journey of the people who travel in search of truth. Only visionary people write the accounts of such journey. While writing down the painful account it is too hard to articulate the stories of ecstasy, love and pain. Only people of the heart do it. The chief organizer of Family of the Heart often arranges the meeting in a manner where even the ring of the dove is not left out and new-comers feel honored and highly regarded. Contrary to the character portrayed by Tagore in one of his poems, the members of the Family of Heart have devoted their lives to the betterment of humanity. Nature will preserve their work in history. The members of the Family of the Heart are oblivious to the corridors of power in the capital city of Ontario. Certainly, the centers of power and the glamour of the media do attract them in the beginning; but after having spent a lifetime in their riddles and juggling one realizes that it was nothing more than an illusion. But people of the heart are not lusty or greedy for fame or causing injury to others. They do not believe in parting ways or divisions. They believe in unity and union. A seeker of truth becomes

witness to it. His heart whispers the verses of Bulhay Shah:

"Bulhay Shah, death will not come to me

Who you see lying in the grave, is not me."

Rabia has asked: "What is the relationship between greatness and humbleness?" Dervish has now understood that Rabia does not ask easy questions. Why? Because she is an idealist, exemplary human and a writer. Dervish opines that knowledge has an in-built arrogance and creativity has built in narcissism in it.

Dervish opines that knowledge makes arrogant and creativity carries narcissism. That is why many knowledgeable writers become arrogant and numerous artists turn self-loving and self-centered. Dervish humorously calls them *"Peace be upon me"* On the other hand, writers who protect and groom their hearts alongside their art, nurture themselves as humble and great persons. In this way they are both great writers and great men. But this is not easy, nor can everybody do it. It needs homework, patience, perseverance, silence, seclusion and wisdom. Dervish divided poets and artists into four kinds; Small artist – Small man, Big artist – Small man, Small artist – Great man and Great artist – Great man.

Dervish measures art by the standards of art and humans according to the standards of character. Dervish met many people of character who were not good artists.

Dervish also opines that in doing such homework, teacher and role models play an important role. Dervish is lucky that his Uncle Arif Abdul Mateen loved him and guided him in the areas of literature and ideologies. Since Dervish was a student of literature and psychology he learnt a lot from many writers, poets and scholars.

Dervish urges Rabia to tell him about her meetings with writers, poets and critics, including great writers – small people and small writers – great people. Dervish wishes to learn from her experience as what should be done and what should not be done.

Dervish requests a break from Rabia as his beloved friend "slumber" is inviting him and promising many sweet dreams.

Thirty-First Dream

Pen and Thought Are Not Independent

1st June 2018

O Dervish! Rabia says Salam from Awan Town School – Lahore, Pakistan.

An Iftar cum Dinner has been organized over here by renowned writer Salma Awan. In one of the halls a poetry recital is taking place. In another, Salma Apa is preparing the dinner with the help of her helpers. Sitting in the compound, we can smell the pleasant aroma of frying – Pakoras [traditional pies]. Fruits have been arranged on the table, while the drinks are being prepared. On the right, a few trees are silently smiling. Pedestal fans on the lawn are forcing the trees to smile. Times change quickly, and life goes on. Change is the spice of life. It makes life colorful. Yet for some the same changes bring misery and suffering.

Rabia has just returned from a poetry recital. She cannot praise every recited verse. In this regard, Rabia is quiet. Salma Awan has invited all her friends and senior poets. The female writers include Rabia Rehman (my best friend), Samina Syed, Ambreen Salah Uddin, Tasneem Kousar, Imrana Mushtaq, Neelma Durrani, Neelam Ahmed Bashir and Seema Peeroz. The poets are Eitbar Sajid, Zia ul Hassan, Jawaz Jaafri, Irfan Sadiq, Hussain Sajid and Tariq Chughtai, besides sixty-five other poets and poetesses. Because of Rabia's indifferent attitude, she does not know most of the participants. She is not sociable. She very rarely attends Halqa Arbab e Zouq Lahore meetings.

There are many writers in Lahore who do not like the limelight of social media. Rabia's journey takes place at the whims of fate. She has never desired to go anywhere.

She just makes a wish and leaves it to life to take her there some day. It is like Khalil Gibran's theory of love: "If you love something, set it free..."

The whole experience of Rabia' life is witness that she never got anything for which she struggled, rather she was blessed with those things for which she never worked hard. She feels that if God wishes to give something, none can stop it and if He does not wish to reward, nobody can receive it.

Now the wife of a famous poet of Lahore has joined us. She is praising her husband like a parrot. A traditional Eastern wife must do it, but while doing it she puts the listener into a fix. On the contrary, the Eastern husband is loyal to every woman save his wife. There is a difference between '"owning a woman" and "keeping a woman." Here the man has learnt to 'keep a woman.' He cares about two women: his mother and his daughter. He loves his wife in old age. When he falls in love with her he also realizes that he is getting old.

Rabia has suddenly recalled John M. Guttmann's famous book, *The Seven Principles for making Marriage work.* He has written the seven principles of a successful marriage:

> *First Principle:* Be aware what your partner likes. You can if only do it you know about it. You should know his or her favorite food, color and dress.

> *Second Principle:* You should know about his sensitivities. Never hurt the feelings of your spouse, take care of them as you would your own feelings.

> *Third Principle:* Praise the good qualities of your spouse in front of him/ her and in front of others as well. It provides positive energy.

Fourth Principle: Take care of small things about your partner. They may look small, but it is most essential principle of a happy married life.

Fifth Principle: You need to understand that every human is unique. He or she is different from you. If the person is different in his or her thinking, their opinion would also be different from yours. That does not warrant his or her rejection. He or she is right from his or her point of view. This should be accepted.

Sixth Principle: Problems that can be solved together and issues that have no solution must be faced together. After all the problems belong to both.

Seventh Principle: Tasks must be listed. Both partners should divide them and work on them together for their common goals.

Rabia thinks that these principles hold for not only the relationship of marriage, but also for any other relationship. Following them can produce excellent results.

Apparently trivial tips can transform a relationship. Here the Iftar cum dinner is almost ready. The birds are happily chirping that Muslims are going to break their fast. Fasting is an exercise to acquire self-control and self-discipline. This also improves the function of the stomach and digestive system. It also teaches us to be trustworthy like Prophet Yousef. Nobody could have known had he misused his privacy with Aziz's woman.

Rabia liked the way Dervish categorized the artists. In Rabia's view there is yet another group of artists who perhaps should not be called by that name. Rabia feels good that her friend (Dervish) was not destined for Lahore. Life took him to a land where he is free, his thought is free and above all his pen is free. Lahore's literary history is enviable, was Rabia's opinion since her childhood, but as she grew up she changed her opinion about it. Thought and the pen are not yet free. They are constrained chains of either society or the family.

Rabia wishes to tell Dervish a recent story that occurred just before Ramadhan. It is about a friend and writer Farhat Parveen. She is nowadays an active member of the Cancer Care and Research Centre Lahore. The other day she had invited a few friends over High Tea at her place. The hospital is providing free treatment to cancer patients, especially for breast cancer. On the occasion, the founding member of the hospital, Dr. Shahryar showed a heart-touching movie to the guests. While delivering his talk he made a very powerful statement: "Perhaps the pen has lost its power."

Rabia and Beena Goindi did not agree with that. Both were of the view that the ways of expression and the readers have changed, but the pen is still powerful.

O Dervish! Rabia requests to leave the letter here. There were many things to write about but Rabia's wish that the letter should be written about the Iftar Dinner has been fulfilled. She is happy about it.

The fragrance of the Lady of the Night is wafting everywhere since evening. It will fill the night till morning.

Rabia's Allah be with Dervish. Goodbye.

Thirty-Second Dream

Man – Woman Friendship

3rd June 2018

Dervish says Salam to Rabia who lives far off but in fact very close to him!

Dervish feels immensely pleased to learn that his dialogue and exchange of letters is continuing with Rabia who lives ten thousand miles away. This exchange of letters emits a fragrance of a true friendship. In one of the letters, Rabia revealed the secret of this friendship: "This friendship is not between a man and woman, it is rather between two humans." Dervish not only agrees with Rabia but would like to add to it: "This is friendship is between two humans who are writers as well as the seekers of the truth."

Dervish is not sure as what Rabia thinks about it, but he is quite certain that his friendship with Rabia would not be possible, had he not done his "home work." Today he would like to share it with Rabia.

When Dervish lived in the East, a friend of him once asked: "Is the friendship between a woman and a man possible without romance and a sexual relationship?" He replied: "Yes. It is possible, but it needs a special man and woman, ordinary people cannot do that." Dervish's friend did not seem in agreement. He said he had never found any such couple in the East.

Dervish could not test his dream and his idea of befriending a woman in the suffocated and frustrated society of the East. However, when Dervish moved to and settled in the West he was introduced to Donna. At that point in time Donna was a teacher in a school for children with special needs. Where she later became Principal. Dervish found Donna a sincere and empathetic person and they became friends. They talked for hours, hung out and dined together. Dervish used to tell Donna all about the Eastern society and Donna would enlighten Dervish about the Western culture.

Once the two sailed to a French island, they rented a room but slept in separate beds as friends. After that, Dervish felt confident that he could act upon his idea of befriending a woman without having physical relationship. Dervish was proud of this friendship. What happened next? A few narrow-minded people became jealous of their friendship. There were rumors about Donna around town. Dervish was hurt. He was sad that some people were eyeing their friendship with doubt.

One day Dervish told Donna, "I have lot of respect for you. I do not want that you should be defamed due to this friendship. If you wish, we can call off the friendship." Donna smiled and replied, "Our friendship is founded on sincerity and our conscience is clear. We should not worry about what people would say. Dervish was impressed by her moral courage and boldness. "One day I will be married, and my husband will accept our friendship. This jealousy and bad-mouthing are only momentary. All the rumors will subside." Dervish did not believe what Donna had said but he remained quiet. After completing his education in psychiatry at St. John's Dervish moved to Whitby where he started his practice in psychotherapy. Despite moving away, his friendship with Donna prevailed with same warmth.

One day he received a call from Donna revealing that she had fallen in love with a man named Ian and she wanted to marry him. She wanted Dervish to meet Ian and approve him as her husband. So, Donna and Ian came to Whitby to stay with him for a couple of days. Dervish was impressed by Ian's manner and thinking and endorsed him. He approved of their marriage. Dervish and Ian also became good friends. Ian became comfortable enough to be candid with Dervish; he told Dervish: "When Donna asked me that to go to meet Dervish, I was worried. I thought perhaps Donna wanted to get my psycho-analyzed. Then I realized that 'Dervish as friend of Donna' was more important than his being a psychotherapist."

Thus, Dervish participated in Donna-Ian marriage as a friend. On the day of their marriage, Dervish recalled Donna's prediction. It had proved true.

Dervish's friendship with Donna was beginning of his "homework." After Donna, Dervish befriended a colleague Anne, who happened to be an atheist. Then came Hildy who came from a Jewish family. After a while Dervish became a friend to Angela who came from Trinidad. She was a nurse and a religious person who sang in the choir at her church. Such friendships proved that Dervish's friendship with women was blind to any race, language, color or religion. But all these female friends were from the West. Whenever, Dervish tried to befriend an Eastern woman it ended with issues. But as luck would have it, Dervish met an Eastern woman. His friendship with Zahra Naqvi was another kind of homework. At their very first meeting Zahra Naqvi told Dervish, "Dervish! I wish to be your friend." "Why?" Dervish asked, smiling. Zahra explained, "I have read your book, *Love, Sex and Woman*. You wrote that whenever you desired to befriend an Eastern woman, her father, brother, husband or son would doubt the relation, leading it into a bitter ending. I assure you that our friendship will remain un-challenged by any of my male relative." This is how Zahra and Dervish became friends. Their friendship is still intact. After the friendship with an Eastern woman, Dervish gained confidence and made more Eastern female friends. This was a detailed account of Dervish's homework, while living in the East. This is what touches Dervish about Rabia. That is the reason Dervish says: "The credit of their friendship goes to Rabia."

Dervish is excited today. He has started a new project; "In Search of Wisdom." This is a TV program telecast with a co-anchor friend Dr. Baland Iqbal. The son of Himayat Ali Shaer, Dr. Baland Iqbal is a physician and writer. In each episode Dervish and Iqbal will discuss one philosopher and his book to let people know what pearls of wisdom had been given to the world by these scholars. To prepare for this project, Dervish read the biographies of fifty philosophers and about a hundred books. He wishes to introduce these philosophers and their works to the masses in simple language. To start with, Dervish wrote an article about the Chinese philosophers Confucius and Lao - Tzu.

Having done that Dervish is very pleased. Whenever Dervish engages in creative work, the child sleeping inside him is awakened and politely demands some sweet or an ice-cream. Now Dervish asks leave from Rabia to entertain the baby so that he cooperates with him next time. It would keep his amazement intact. Dervish thinks it mandatory for any poet or writer that his inner curious child must stay alive.

What has Rabia to say about it?

Thirty-Third Dream

We All are Foreigners

4th June 2018

Hello Dervish, fragrant breezes coming from a foreign land present Salam!

Dervish's country is a foreign land for Rabia. The same is true for Dervish where Rabia dwells. No matter in what country a person lives, he is a traveler who passes through this world like a stranger. A poet has described this phenomenon in a famous Hindi song: -

PerdesioN say na akhiaN milana

PerdesioN ko hay ikk din jana

Never cast an eye at the travelers

The travelers have to leave one day

O Dervish! We too must leave this world one day. So, in a way we too are travelers here, the travelers of the journey of this very life. The travels that encounter 'wonders' never end. Rabia fully agrees to the philosophy of 'wonders' proffered by Dervish in his previous letter. Rabia got disconnected with Dervish for a while. Nevertheless, such disruptions are caused by nature, these take creativity further. Moreover, the creativity becomes a rainbow of colors in solitude.

Once again, Rabia wishes to tell Dervish the story of her early education. Except for four years, Rabia was educated in the co-education system. For most of that time one of her brothers was Rabia's class-mate, till he moved to another college. Then came her university life when Rabia started to write prose. After that, life left Rabia with few choices. She was in a swirl of emotions, feelings, paper and the pen. In short, Rabia was entrapped by the oppressions of time. Life was left behind somewhere. The turmoil of confinement against her wishes was so severe that she could not cope with the situation. Rabia waited for the bad days to pass. But time had come to a standstill. It was hard to endure. Rabia often could hear the echo of her favorite teacher Asghar Nadeem Syed's words: "Write and write so much that your words should start speaking…"

Rabia took to writing short stories. These were published in renowned literary magazines of Pakistan. Other than that, Rabia passed her time by either watching movies or reading books. Other than 'action' movies, Rabia liked themes such as art, classical and romantic. German and Iranian films too left an imprint on Rabia's mind.

A few years passed in this inertia. Soon Rabia was nicknamed as "Al Raba" in literary circles and among friends. The short story became her preferred medium. At least the Urdu story readers knew her well. On one of those static days, Rabia was called by a literary publisher with an offer to compile a modern-age Encyclopedia of Afsanas. She agreed, although perplexed by the lack of any written agreement. She was also required to work quietly. She worked day and night for seven long years. However, the project took an adverse turn near the end. Suffice it to say that Rabia's Allah saved her from a nervous breakdown. In fact, it turned into a breakthrough. The proud and arrogant Zuleikha and Pharaohs of our time always forget that there is a God above, the God of Musa and Yusaf. By God, He is there! Has Dervish ever witnessed the elegance of Yousef's and Musa's God? Rabia is witnessing it even now.

Over here the summer is at its peak. It's a June evening. Rabia is sitting on her terrace to receive the cool breeze. Air-conditioned rooms cannot give such freshness. There is peace, joy and serenity all around. Two times will meet in a while; grey clouds are gathering on the western horizon to provide a curtain to hide the union of both times.

O Dervish! I beg your pardon for having dived into the stream of my unconscious mind.

Coming back to the project – the compilation story of the Encyclopedia. Rabia embarked upon the work from Great Britain. Mirza Amjad had written an anthology named: *Famous Literary Personalities of Great Britain* The book was in the completion stage. Through Mirza Amjad, Rabia got connected to the literary circles of Europe. The work that had commenced at a slow and steady pace now spread to the entire world at great speed. In those days, the communication applications like WhatsApp were not yet appeared. However, Viber and Skype did exist but were limited to America. Countries like Pakistan were still deprived off such fast and cheap means of video and audio chats. Nevertheless, email did exist. Then there was an issue of the time difference. The work would have become onerous, had it not become Rabia's passion. Rabia was able to connect to over four hundred Urdu Writers all over the world. It opened a new window in Rabia's mind, a candle of love in the secluded darkness of Rabia's heart. There were occasional mistakes — sometimes a slight error in the address resulted in emails being sent to another person who in reply would congratulate Rabia for doing such a massive piece of work.

During that time, Rabia came across many immigrants in foreign countries who were in a state of intense nostalgia. They wished to hear all about Pakistan and Pakistanis. In the end, Rabia connected to Pakistani and Indian writers but never made any male friend. Over here there cannot be any friendship between two humans, it has to be between a woman and a man. They are like Adam and Eve — still naked despite being thrown out of the Garden of Eden. Perhaps they are not yet fully developed as humans yet.

Lust is overwhelming in married people as well. It does not stop at a wife, a friend or a girlfriend. Men do not befriend humans — they befriend female bodies. Even education has not brought about much change in people's attitudes. Over here we have not accepted woman as human. The woman is a sex doll — her brain works at the lowest, instinctive level. The strings of a woman's life are held in the hands of men who called themselves Mehrams [forbidden to marry in Islamic Sharia] and Na-Mehrams [allowed to marry in Islamic Sharia]. Na-Mehrams often entice young girls to satisfy their lust in the garb of love. Such love affairs leave young women with psychological disorders or sometimes pregnant. Such unwanted pregnancies either result in abortions or infants dumped in garbage heaps. The men use women's bodies like wild dogs or cheetahs, to render them not worthy of marriage. Such use of a woman body by a man to comfort himself is called "love-making." Here, the woman of today is either a mother or a harlot. The brothels have been banned, but the prostitution has moved to the homes of the so-called honorable elite. In this society, a woman is used by men like a commodity, a sex toy who has no choice of her own. The man of this society likes to play with this toy to his heart's content. He is driven by his male organ, his desire and above all, his lust, no matter how much it hurts the woman emotionally and physically. The men over here boast about their hooks, flirtations and traps. A man can even hand over his "girlfriend" to another friend as he does not care about respect, honor or the feelings of another man's daughter or sister. While doing all this, the men of today do not care about the age of the female. The recent case of child sex abuse amply endorses this point.

O Dervish! You will agree that, if you want to drink a cup of tea, you would visit a nearby cafeteria. But if you knock on every door and ask for tea, does it make any sense? Does it look nice for that matter? The men of this society don't want to "pay for tea" in a decent hotel. They would rather beg for a cup of tea from here and there. Women are equally desperate for men. Suffice it to say that men and women in this society are enslaved to lust, sex and pleasure. {Rabia's speculations}

The easiest way to hook a girl in this society is a promise of marriage. It works both for the girl and her parents. The parents here raise their daughters to believe that their would-be-husband is a hero who would take her to Heaven right away. In fact, the same hero shatters all her dreams before and after the marriage. The girl breaks in the hands of her hero like a glass-toy.

Currently here, the rhythmic breezes are so soothing. The dawn is about to break, the softly blowing wind is telling her story. The fragrance says that it's coming from a far-off land. The country where it dropped the rains of love and friendship.

Rabia's struggle to survive in the man-dominated, lecherous environment was Rabia's homework (as Dervish calls it). Rabia has tried to share her point of view with Dervish in the best possible manner. She does not want to leave her favorite song being sung by Jamun twigs in the wind. Neither does she wish to get away from nature, creativity and the road ahead but the epistle is getting a bit long now. Moreover, Rabia has said whatever she had to say to the best of her humble ability.

O Dervish! A crow is calling nearby, and a dove is also chirping to announce the arrival of day. Rabia wishes to proceed on the journey of dreams. Life is not permitting her to understand "The Forty Rules of Love." Her slumber might make it possible.

O Dervish! Goodnight.

Thirty-Fourth Dream

Every Life Needs a Rule

8th June 2018

O Dervish! Please accept the belated greeting of a bright morning here.

I turned up late this time as my life was in a learning process. My days were baking few rules of life in the oven of experience. Life is a strange question and the answer is even stranger. Humans are ignorant beings. They assume every answer is a rule and measure the rest of life with this new rule. Whereas, every man-made rule gives birth to another question. Hence, the rules add up to humans themselves. One rule cannot answer the questions pertaining to all men. Every life needs its own set of rules. Every human being has his or her own key that opens the inner lock. Many humans spend their lives with a closed person because they do not have the key to open that person up. Sometimes, the other person holds the key, but most of the time they both end up without opening each other and ultimately depart to the next world. Uncle Ghalib has rightly said:

> *Marr kay bhi chan Na paya tou kidhar jaengay?*
>
> *Where further will we wander in search of peace?*
>
> *If there was none even after we were deceased*

In fact, we won't go anywhere. It is a vicious circle, unending. Humans fear bad times but do not remember them and forget to appreciate the good times. Moreover, they are not even contented with a steady state, forgetting that neither the dark days nor the bright ones were in their control. Nevertheless, there are momentary ups and downs, fetters on peoples' feet making them realize that the real power lies somewhere else. A few days ago, Rabia read the findings of a psychologist who used two metaphors for two kind of humans; Basket and Diaper.

Basket: These individuals grow your creative abilities further. They look out for you and make good friends. This all takes place unconsciously.

Diaper: These individuals weaken your creativity, natural talents and energy to grow. They bring turbulence in your life.

They are like two magnets that repel each other.

O Dervish! It may be a pleasant coincidence that Rabia had the opportunity to meet and observe both kinds. Rabia is of the view that every person has a filter attached to his life that keeps screening people. At the end of the day you are left with only those people who you are comfortable with.

Like-minded people pass through the filter. The people who stay around become your clan, the clan of comfort or soul mates. They remain restless when away from each other and seek bliss while in the chemistry of proximity. Such chemistry is a scientific phenomenon. Science is working more on it. It will come out with further revelations. A day will come when soul, mind and psyche will also have different meanings altogether.

Dervish in his last letter had asked Rabia about her "homework." Rabia calls it helplessness. This condition cannot change despite concerted efforts. The compulsions, be they social or family, are attached to a person invisibly right from his birth. They stay with a person like a body's natural fragrance. No amount of washing, bathing or any other concoction works to take away this smell.

You accept it as an essential part of life or reject it. If you accept, it becomes a truth of your life. In case of rejection it becomes a constant problem, a question or a padlock. Now you need a key to unlock it. The search for the key becomes yet another journey.

Now things happen in your life, strange incidents take place and you encounter many twists and turns, ups and downs. Then either you find the key one day, or the journey continues. At times the key holder comes very close but unknowingly moves away without inserting into the keyhole, leaving your lock to rust for the rest of your life.

To sum up, Rabia did not do any homework. The boat of life that of Moses, took her to unwanted and unknown places. Where she was born was not her choice — neither the surroundings nor the conditions were created by her. She wanted to change but failed. Now she is left with no other option than to accept.

Rabia was her parents' first child. The other siblings were brothers. She was born in a joint family system. Rabia's and her uncles' families lived as one family in Model Town – Lahore. In a way Rabia had eight brothers, Therefore, Rabia was raised with ten male psyches. There were no other girls Rabia's age, either on the maternal or on the parental side. It made her a pampered child.

Time went by fast. Rabia was a grown-up girl when other girls were born in the family. She was not allowed to play with them. Her father did not allow her to mix with other girls, as he wanted to make Rabia a special girl. The isolation turned her into an abnormal child. However, Rabia was lucky enough that she was permitted to play with her brothers and cousins. It made her a sort of tomboy. But later on, she realized that a girl looks more beautiful as a girl. Staying natural is a beauty. It took time however, to revert to femininity. She however, never wavered in her love for her brothers; she thought that manhood and womanhood suit both genders respectively.

Any rebellion against nature causes disorder and discomforts. In times of turbulence and restlessness no rule, philosophy or key works. The circumstances created by nature should be accepted as such. At times, what you consider a 'fault in the stars' has a concealed blessing for you.

O Dervish! Like always, many thoughts remain to be written. The battery of my computer is about to die. I forgot to connect it to the charger.

Goodnight at 6:30 in the morning as it must be night with Dervish. Before placing Dervish into God's protection, Rabia wishes to write a couplet here. She should be pardoned for any mistakes:

Accidents do not occur blind

There are always reasons behind

Thirty-Fifth Dream

Spirituality… Insanity… Creativity

8th June 2018

Adaab to Rabia who lives across the seven seas!

Rabia's letters tell Dervish that she has dived quite deep into the waters of self-awareness. So deep that the coastline and midstream merge to become invisible. Her letters look like a prism, a rainbow that refracts. Its droplets spread seven colors of light when the sun rays hit them. This rainbow is inside Rabia, constantly refracting light on the computer screen or a piece of paper after passing through her pen.

Dervish is gradually concluding that although Rabia and Dervish are two seekers of truth, because of their personalities, experiences and ideologies, they follow different paths. Dervish smiles at the fact that Rabia considers psychological realities in the mirror of spirituality. On the contrary Dervish looks at spiritual experiences through the lens of psychology.

Dervish often thinks his philosophy and world-view might be the outcome of certain experiences he underwent at a very early age. Dervish had written to Rabia in one of his previous letters that when his father, Abdul Basit, suffered from a psychological trauma he was 40, whereas Dervish was only 10 years old. Prior to that his father taught mathematics at Government College Kohat. He was a sophisticated teacher, who was clean-shaven and used to wear an expensive suit and a neck-tie. Abdul Basit was an atheist. On recovering from his breakdown, he resigned from the government job and began teaching at a private high school in Peshawar. During that time he seriously started studying Islam. He researched the Holy Quran, read related religious books and took the path of spirituality. He was a changed man now. From then on, his father ate simple food, wore simple attire and lived a simple life.

People called him a Sufi. The first book that he brought home was *Tazkra tul Aulia* [The Accounts of the Saints.] Dervish for the first time read about Rabia Basri in that book. He was so impressed by the life of Rabia Basri that he wrote an essay on the great saint of Islamic history. The essay was published in a children's magazine. Ah yes! Rabia Basri became a muse for his first creation, like Rabia is acting as muse for these letters.

Dervish strongly feels that he might have been unconsciously motivated by his father's mental crisis to become a psychiatrist to understand the human brain and find cures for its ailments.

After he became a psychiatrist, Dervish had a chance to attend an international conference in Brazil where he read a paper on the psychological issues of immigrants. After that he attended a seminar where he met the experts and research scholars of Iceland. Those researchers had worked with mentally ill patients in the hospital. Their research revealed that the families of such patients had three times the number of creative people (writers, poets, artists and scholars) than the ordinary people. The mind-experts are of the view that insanity and creativity have the same genes. When a creative child has the right environment, he becomes a successful artist. On the contrary, when the environment is not conducive, the person develops a psychological disorder.

The opinion of experts was strengthened in Dervish's mind when he read biographies of great artists. Studying the biographies of poets, writers, artists and scholars, Dervish was astonished to learn that some had even committed suicide during a psychological crisis. Some who ended their own lives were Virginia Woolf,

Sylvia Plath, Ernest Hemmingway and Vincent Van Gogh. There were others who survived their psychological crisis. They, like Dervish's father became spiritual. The biographies revealed to Dervish that inanity, creativity and spirituality were also mystically and mysteriously linked to each other. To understand the mystery of the relationship, Dervish selected three autobiographies: Abu Hameed, Al-Ghazali, Leo Tolstoy and Carl Jung. The three scholars were successful and famous writers in the prime of their youth. Then they realized that their success was in fact materialistic, worldly and superficial. After this realization they passed through a painful psychological crisis. Their creativity was paralyzed, and they were disorientated from routine life. When they recovered, all of them had become spiritual.

To Dervish, it was interesting to note that these philosophers changed their worldview, ideas and philosophies of life altogether.

Ghazali who was once a strong advocate of philosophy turned against it. He suggested that religion and science, philosophy and spirituality are contradictory. He advised Muslims to accept religion and spirituality and reject science and philosophy. Therefore, millions of talented Muslims who followed his theology have rejected science and philosophy over the centuries. Leo Tolstoy who was the author of famous novel, *War and Peace* stopped writing fiction and started preaching Christianity and peace. He suggested to Christians that Christianity was a religion of peace. Many soldiers who followed Tolstoy resigned from the armed forces.

Notwithstanding the above, Carl Jung embraced altogether different. He described his spiritual experiences in his book named *Red Book*. Which was published decades after his death. A copy of the book was given to Dervish by one of his friends, Hildy Abrams. Jung was of the view that religion and science, spirituality and psychology were in fact different facets of one reality. There was no fundamental difference amongst them. It was the point of view that made the difference.

The same reality can be understood from the angle of logic as well as from the angle of intuition. In Jung's point of view, "A spiritual experience was essentially a personal experience. However, it can only acquire universal experience only after it has been proven with scientific and psychological evidence."

Therefore, Jung presented his spiritual experiences after proving them with psychological evidence. He further stated that: "If a scientist, a philosopher and a Sufi are real seekers of truth, despite moving on divergent paths, they would arrive at the same destination." Dervish liked this observation of Jung that, "As a person ages, the experiences of life make him wiser; the person moves beyond and above wealth and fame. He or she knows himself and the mystery of the universe."

The biographies of Ghazali, Tolstoy and Jung helped Dervish to better understand his father and uncle. Dervish is fortunate enough to have acquired traditional love from his maternal family and non-traditional wisdom from his paternal family. Such nourishment nurtured into Dervish a poet, a writer and humanist psychotherapist so that he should serve humanity with compassion.

When Dervish was working on his book *Mysteries of Mysticism* he came to realize that there was a time when spirituality was found only in religious books. But in the past two centuries, the experts in science, medicine and psychology have carried out research on spiritual experiences based on scientific and psychological evidence. Many 21st century secular scholars and scientific researchers believe that spirituality is part of humanity and even people who do not believe in any God or religion can have spiritual experiences. Such experiences can be produced by stimulation of the right temporal lobe of the human brain.

The only difference is that religious people interpret their spiritual experiences through their religions, traditions and connect themselves with religion and God, whereas secular gurus endeavor to analyze such experiences through the human brain, mind, personality and subconscious. Therefore, Dervish expressed his point of view in these words: "Spirituality is part of humanity, not divinity."

Dervish feels more attached to science and psychology, whereas Rabia relates to literature and spiritualism. Their paths may be different, but their destination is the same. Both are sincere in their cause and in their search. They respect each other. That is the foundation of their long-distance creative friendship. Dervish although knows that Rabia carried out a marathon research on Urdu Afsana [Urdu Short Story] but he has yet to learn which literary personalities she interacted with and who impressed her.

Dervish also wishes to share an account of his meeting with a literary personality. Dervish may be selfish, but he is confessing his selfishness while writing the letter. Dervish was oblivious to the Goddess of slumber who has been knocking at his bedroom for quite a while. He requests a leave from Rabia.

Thirty-Sixth Dream

Sensitivity is a Blissful Ailment

20th June 2018

O Dervish! Rabia says good morning, and good evening from a misfit society.

Rabia is impressed by Dervish's last letter but cannot reply right away as she has suddenly fallen sick. At this moment her heart craves to read a book, but the severe pain is oozing out from her eyes. Being sensitive is a blissful ailment. The one who inflicts pain is enslaved to his carnal desires. He doesn't understand that wanderers and dervishes are not hurt by physical distress. This all is meaningless to them. The source of their peace as well as their turbulence lies somewhere else. They are travelers through a different valley. They are souls of a different clan. They live by the heart, not by the body.

O Dervish! What you called your selfishness is in fact bearing out a pearl of wisdom. But the pearl yearns to come out. It is ready to benefit others.

Ah, Dervish! You have also urged Rabia to write her memoir of her meetings with artists. Rabia's raindrop has not yet turned into a pearl. It needs more time. But Rabia gives her consent to Dervish to write his account of his meetings with artists. Rabia wants to read about that. She also sees motivation which might turn her creative clay into gold.

O Dervish! Life is very strange. You need to be stonehearted. You must be a heedless person to stay cool. What makes Rabia gloomy today? This evening she watched a painful story on television. The news broke that a girl was hanged by her father. The honor killing was done on allegations of adultery. The girl's mother was shown shedding crocodile tears and begging for justice.

But neither was the father embarrassed, nor the mother gloomy. Both portrayed themselves as heroes of the episode. Appearing on television was enough justice for them. The daughters of such parents should die.

Another taboo of her society that pinches Rabia's sensitive heart is the *Maan* [claim or right]. A woman of Eastern society uses this custom to the best of her advantage. If she is a wife she would say, "I have a claim on my husband. After all he is my earthly god". If she is a mother, she would say, "If a mother does not have any 'right' on son who would do it after all". The same exploitation is often done by sisters to brothers. Rabia considers these claims to be emotional blackmailing. The men of her society are victims of this exploitation. To her a relationship is about sincerity, love and compassion. When it is exploited by the claims and rights, it loses its very innocence and beauty. Rabia is fed up with this debasement.

Dervish has asked Rabia who impressed her the most. Well! Rabia, doesn't get impressed by people in that sense. She just meets them. To her the meaning of being impressed has changed. However, she might have answered the question, had Dervish asked it ten years ago. Things appear accurate neither from a long distance nor from too much proximity. However, Rabia is more impressed by the attributes than the people themselves. She is touched by innocence and modesty, be they of faces, feelings or love. These are very pure attributes. She stays there to feel the bliss of such feelings. But when these attributes are taken away she moves away.

Having said that, Rabia will wait for the letter from Dervish containing his memoirs.

The night is turning into day over here. Rabia has so much to talk about. Life holds many questions. Rabia wishes to get out of here. She wants to live somewhere

where people spend their lives as they wish. A dwelling where people prize others' talents and respect each other. A society where people do not exploit relationships over monetary benefits. A land where people greet each other with smiling faces.

Has Dervish ever observed how meaningless life is? It is like a building that stands on the pillars of a few momentary decisions. It is these pillars that affect the entire life the most. All other things are nothing more than cement, sand, gravel and the labor required to construct it. Lucky are those people whose pillars of decision are firm enough to raise a sound building of life the dwellers of which feel safe and protected.

Alright, Dervish! Kindly grant me leave as my pain is once again becoming unbearable. Over here, psychiatrists and physicians have only diagnosis of such agony: insensitivity. Well Rabia cannot do that. It would be like putting a sewage line into spring water.

A peaceful morning says goodnight.

Thirty-Seventh Dream

A Meeting with Joginder Paul

11th June 2018

Dervish presents Salam to Rabia's dreams and ideas.

Dervish during his life span had many opportunities to meet and interview numerous poets, writers and scholars, a few of whom greatly impressed him. One of those was Joginder Paul. Dervish wishes to share his account of his meeting with Paul.

During one of his travels to India, Dervish went to stay with Sharib Rudolvi. Professor Rudolvi is an important name in the field of Urdu language and literature. Sharib Rudolvi told Dervish, "I have invited numerous literary friends this evening so that you can meet them." The important names amongst the guests were Irtaza Kareem, Qamar Raees and Joginder Paul. Hearing Paul's, Dervish was excited as he was an important name in Urdu Afsana. In the evening, Sharib said: "I have invited him but am not sure he will make it as he lives forty kilometers from here and does not drive a car." "I hope he can come," Dervish's heart whispered. "Please tell me something about Joginder Paul," Dervish requested his host.

Sharib said, "I once went to see Paul. I urged him to translate an English novel into Urdu. When I told him about the book, he politely declined, saying that he was resigning his job. 'Why so?' I inquired. He explained: "I want to write a novel about blind people, who live under one roof – their loves, rivalries and friendships. I need complete focus and concentration for the novel. Such a creative project cannot be done alongside a job. Therefore, I have decided to quit my job to work on the book "

While Dervish and Sharib Rudolvi were talking, the door opened and a white haired elderly man in *salwar qamiz* and a blue sweater entered the room. He headed straight to Dervish and said, "I am Joginder Paul." He hugged Dervish like an old friend. He continued, "Come sit with me. I am especially here to meet you and talk for a while."

Dervish felt as if he had touched an ocean of love. Joginder Paul was so kind, caring and passionate that Dervish felt as if he had known him for ages.

Joginder Paul said to Dervish, "I read your novelette *Toota Huwa Admi* [*A Broken Man*]. I appreciate your courage. You make wonderful use of words to express yourself. These days many writers use words to conceal themselves. I am here to congratulate you." He paused for a moment and resumed "A passion, a spirit and a certain sacrifice are required to create fiction. You own all of them." Then Joginder Paul presented Dervish with an autograph copy of his book *Khulla* [Opened].

After dinner Dervish asked Paul, "How would you describe the process of creating a story?" Paul replied, "To me, writing a story is like driving a car in the fog. The reader is my co-traveler in my car. As we move forward, new turns, new roads are revealed to me as well as to the reader. Writing and reading a story is a slow and steady process of revelation. I do not like those writers whose stories right from beginning tells you the roads, the turns and the destination."

He again paused then said, "A genuine writer is perpetually looking for new approaches and is ready to present novel experiences in an innovative manner. Innovations in writing styles are crucial, or else you get into a cycle of clichéd writing".

When leaving, Paul embraced Dervish and said, "This was a short meeting. When you come to India next time, see to it that you spend an entire day with me. Then we will talk at length." Although Dervish's meeting with Joginder Paul was short, it was far better than many lengthy meetings with numerous writers.

Dervish wished to share the account of his meeting with Rabia because she is also a story writer and while writing the accounts of her dreams, she is undertaking a creative experience.

Thirty-Eighth Dream

Letters Make a Painting

12ᵗʰ June 2018

Dervish presents Salam to the night-vigilant Rabia!

For quite a while Dervish has been thinking that his and Rabia's letters are turning into a painting. With each passing day, the colors are getting sharper. When Dervish carefully reads her letters, he can see the seven colors of rainbow in them. He also knows that there are other colors still invisible to him.

The first color is of a creative dialogue.

The second color depicts colloquy.

The third color shows a worldview.

The fourth color manifests literature.

The fifth color denotes spirituality.

The sixth color represents psychology.

The seventh color highlights the friendship.

The last color dominates all others, as friendship holds sincerity, ownership, respect and regard, besides the process of learning from each other. Dervish is impressed by Rabia's prose. It contains poetry, fluency and wisdom. This dialogue is a discourse of two writer-friends who are traveling in search of Truth.

For all these years Dervish has been dreaming of exchanging letters with Rabia as he knew that the genre of letters has a wider canvas than the Ghazal, Poem, Short Story and Play. When thoughts, emotions, ideas and expressions are enveloped into the folds of the conscious and unconscious mind, they become different from other genres of fiction. Dervish is of the view that Letter Fiction has not been given the place in Urdu literature it deserved. Letters have been ignored, considering them a private scribble. Ghalib's letters were valued in Urdu Literature but again those letters were in a way, a monologue.

Dervish had always wished to create a two-way dialogue, but he needed another writer for that. In fact, Dervish did try it with one or two writers who became Rabia for exchanging letters, but the discourse ceased due to some unavoidable circumstances. Dervish had never thought that one day he would find a real Rabia sitting ten thousand miles away who would turn his dream into reality. Dervish is immensely happy exchanging knowledge and literary, social and ideological views with Rabia. He thanks Rabia for this creative dialogue from the bottom of his heart.

Dervish has never met Rabia, yet he feels a literary connection with her. One of the definitions of friendship is that "the friends highlight the best attributes of each other". Today in the East, the friendship between a man and a woman is scarce if not non-existent.

What does Rabia think about it?

Thirty-Ninth Dream

Wisdom of Women

13th June 2018

From across the seven seas, under seven heavens and amid countless galaxies Rabia says 'hi' to Dervish.

The wind of Dervish's renowned Green Zone Therapy has already travelled from West to East. Rabia too is eager to know about it.

Rabia enjoyed reading the accounts of his meeting with Joginder Paul. We too (in one sense) are talking about sight-impaired people.

Rabia is very happy that despite the contrast of ideas, knowledge, thinking and experiences, Dervish did not make it a point of ego. The use of the word "wisdom" with "Rabia" was a wonderful surprise for her. It made Rabia smile. In the East it looks strange to see "wise woman" written anywhere. However, you often find the phrases like "foolish woman" or "insane woman". Over here, you neither talk wisdom nor expect wisdom from a woman. If you hear of a wise woman somewhere, your young girls must stay away from her. Her wisdom must stay inside the walls of her house and directed only at her husband. We have women for sex. Even from a far-off distance, men's carnal instinct sends strong signals to a woman with the speed of light. She feels so harassed that more often than not, she loses her wits. This was just a glimpse of the ambience where Rabia dwells. In such a suffocated and perverted environment a friendship like that of Rabia and Dervish is scarce as well as precious. Here, such friendship takes place in old age, when the partners are physically weak, in need of vitality medications. In Rabia's society, respect is granted to a woman only when she has aged enough to no longer be sexually attractive. At that age she is expected to be respectful and respectable.

O Dervish! This society is bunch of psychopaths who have created the atmosphere of a madhouse. Every home needs a psychiatrist. No doubt the women are intelligent, but their intellect is utilized mostly on family politics. Most entertainment channels in Asian countries base their Soaps on family politics. These serials get higher ratings than any other programs. That is another proof of a woman's wisdom.

Rabia is happy to be working on a project with a person of a magnanimous nature and an open mind. Rabia loves such people but unfortunately does not find them around here. You can follow either your heart or your intellect. Woman can be enticed through both to satisfy a man's lust. There is no other reason for befriending her at least if she is sexually attractive. But again, Rabia also believes that nothing is impossible.

In Rabia's society, modesty is applied only to women. It's considered her ornament, whereas men feel proud of being vulgar. Rather their lechery is a symbol of their manhood. The prophet Yousef is not liked much. But at the same time, they describe themselves as the second Yousef to impress woman. Then they describe their past affairs to their friends. They protest that they were innocent like Yousef who became a helpless victim of wicked Zuleikha. Some say they were raped by so and so woman, as if they were simple-minded clueless and feeble. Such stories are told by women as well. So ridiculous. They have no idea that Rabia feels pity for them.

In one of Dervish's previous letters Rabia read that a conducive environment encourages artists. Rabia thinks otherwise. She is of the view that a non-conducive environment at times forges an artist. However, Rabia agrees with Dervish's theory that insanity, creativity and spirituality have the same set of genes.

Rabia feels elated that she and Dervish despite taking different paths are travelers to the same destination. They are the seekers of truth.

Rabia would like to hear few stories of Dervish's memorable patients. But for now, she would like to answer Dervish's question about her marriage. Ah! Yes. That is a question to which Rabia does not have a ready answer. She thinks marriage is a gamble that could turn out to be pleasant or unpleasant. But it did not occur in her life. As young child, whenever Rabia attended a marriage the bride and groom looked like cartoons. At that time, she promised to herself that she would not become a cartoon if she ever got a chance to marry. When it comes to marriage it should remain a simple affair. But that time never arrived for her.

Rabia did not agree to the myth that only beautiful women produce cute babies. She believed that it all depended on the strength of genes.

Rabia considered herself a traditional woman who would become a wife one day. She would produce children and change multiple diapers. If she complained to her mother about her husband, the reply would be, "Look, Daughter, all men are like that. Your Dad was like that too." She was ready to sacrifice her freedom like any other girl.

What Raba is today was unimaginable in her youth. We in this society raise the girl with such traditional concepts: "This is not your home. Your home is that of your husband. He is your prince." A woman has no home. She remains a stranger even in her home. Her would-be husband is portrayed as a Superman who would take on anyone. In fact, he doesn't prove to be even a man. Such myths are then transferred to the next generation, so on and so forth…

O Dervish! We will continue the conversation. Right now, Rabia must talk to her Allah. After all the contact must be maintained with the Creator so that there are no apologies later. The contact is first step toward the true love.

Rabia would like to go to sleep with the hope that slumber takes her to the valley of peaceful sleep like it does to Dervish. Rabia wanders the countless valleys when she lies down to sleep. Then one of the valleys takes her into the lap of sleep.

Goodnight, Dervish.

Fortieth Dream

Green Zone Philosophy

13th June 2018

Dervish says Adaab to Rabia, the knower of the secrets of solitude, silence and wisdom!

While reading Rabia's letters Dervish dives into the depths of the philosophical oratory and wishes to answer one letter with three letters. But the number and length of letters restrains him. Dervish puts it like this: "Series of letters is like a train rolling on a mutually built track and fast heading toward unknown destinations."

Dervish has never had such a marathon dialogue with any friend, especially a pen friend whom he had never met. But in this case, it's quite different. Despite writing a good deal it feels like Dervish should write more.

While writing letters to Rabia, Dervish wears different hats: a poet or a writer or a humanist. Today, he wishes to put on the hat of a 'therapist' so that he can share a few professional experiences.

Dervish apologizes to Rabia in advance as this letter may become a bit long and she might have to read it in more than one sitting.

Studying psychology for nine long years, five in Pakistan and four in Canada, Dervish learnt that most doctors and psychiatrists use medication to treat psychiatric patients. Dervish wanted to change this trend. He wished to treat patients through therapy, relying on minimum of medication. Dervish had a professional vision of designing a self-help program to benefit his patients.

How did Dervish's dream turn into reality? He will tell this story to Rabia.

Being a poet and a writer, Dervish is quite aware of those moments in time when the seed of an innovative idea, a fresh thought, or a deeper wisdom is sown in the field of the mind and slowly grows into a fruit-tree. Dervish also knows the value of those moments. Dervish experienced a similar creative moment in his clinic.

Dervish was seeing a couple, Bill and Nancy. Bill was angry and sarcastic towards his wife. He would humiliate and abuse her. Nancy initially tried to pacify her husband, but finally threatened to take their son and leave him unless he consented to counseling. Bill agreed to see their family doctor who referred them to Dervish.

At the first session with Dervish, Bill said that he loved his wife and could not imagine a breakup. He further revealed that he had been raised in a family where his father used to not only humiliate but also hit his mother. His mother was always scared of his father. In one of the interviews Bill talked affectionately about his son whom he loved a lot. Dervish asked Bill; "What do you wish your son to become when he grows up?" "A prince," Bill replied spontaneously. "If you want your son to grow up to be a prince, you must treat his mother like a queen. He can never become a prince if you treat his mother like a maid." On another day, Dervish asked Bill, "If you love your wife then why do you criticize her?" Bill explained, "Something goes wrong with me. A trivial thing riles me up and I go hyper. I say such awful things that I feel embarrassed later. The next day I feel ashamed and promise to myself that I won't do it again. But few days later, I do the same thing. I can't remember how long I've been doing this".

Dervish looked into Bill's eyes and asked him, "What do you do when you are driving a car and the traffic light turns yellow?

"I press the accelerator," Bill replied.

"Why?" Dervish asked.

"I am always in a hurry to get to the office or pick my son from the baby sitter or get back home."

Dervish said, "An intelligent person hits the break, not the accelerator, on seeing a yellow light and does not move forward until it turns green. Whenever you are angry, you are psychologically in a Yellow Zone. You should stop and leave the room. When you do not stop while in that state of anger, you move into the Red Zone and lose control of yourself. You should wait until you come back to your Green Zone." Having listened to Dervish, Bill promised to act upon his advice.

Two weeks later when Nancy came to see Dervish, she said, "What a miracle! Bill is improving a lot." Dervish was pleased that Bill was serious about his treatment. Since he loved his wife and son and did not wish to lose them, he was struggling to become a good father and a kind husband. After a few months of treatment Bill improved further and ultimately learned to control his anger.

After treating Bill, Dervish reflected upon the concept of Green, Yellow and Red Zone. He realized that there was a useful psychological comparison with traffic lights. Dervish applied the concept with several couples with whom it worked well. The concept continued to grow in Dervish's mind like a seed which eventually became a tree to bear fruit. The Green Zone philosophy turned into a self-help philosophy. Dervish wrote many books on this philosophy and also developed a website: *www.greenzoneliving.com*. The foundation of Green Zone Philosophy revolves around 3 Zones: Green Zone, Yellow Zone and Red Zone.

- When we are happy and enjoying our life, we are in our Green Zone.

- When we are little perturbed, a little worried or a little angry, we are in our Yellow Zone.

- When we lose our temper under the influence of anger or we are gloomy due to a difficult situation, we are in our Red Zone.

Then there are three **"R's:" Recognizing, Recovering and Restraining.**

- *Recognizing:* We can learn when we move from one Zone to another.

- *Recovering*: We learn how to revert to our Green Zone from the Red or Yellow Zone.

- *Restraining*: We acquire the ability to learn what circumstances and which people push us to Red Zone.

Using this ability, we become attuned to and ready to deal with situations so that we don't lose control. Green Zone philosophy says: Green Zone People ACT, Red Zone People REACT. Following the above principles, we begin to spend more and more time in Green Zone. Dervish advices his patients to keep a Green Zone Diary for a few weeks. Every night before going to bed they should write an account of the last twenty-four hours. How many hours were they in the Red Zone, Green Zone and Yellow Zone? And what were they doing while in the respective Zones? This is how they become aware of their psychological changes and can learn to overcome them.

- **3 Ways to Deal with Conflicts:** When his patients start to spend their most of their time in their Green Zones, Dervish asks them how to make a list of their relationships and asks them to tell him the Zones of the people in each relationship. He tells them how to bring those people into the Green Zone from Yellow and Red Zones.

- The first method is to resolve. In this method affected people resolve the conflict through mutual dialogue and bring the relationship back to the Green Zone.

- The second method is to dissolve. If one person refuses to take responsibility for his part in the relationship, the other can abandon him.

- The third method is to mediate. In this approach the two people seek the help of a third person who can help resolve their disputes. The third person could be a friend, relative or therapist.

The next facet of the Green Zone Philosophy is the systems in which an individual finds himself most of the time. Like people who are in Green, Yellow and Red Zones, systems also occupy in one of these zones. Most people live in three systems: Family System, Work System and Social System. Dervish tells his patients that systems are very strong. If a system is constantly in the Red Zone, it's very difficult for an individual to stay in their Green Zone.

The next "R" of the Green Zone Philosophy is: "The three Roads to a GREEN ZONE LIFESTYLE." Dervish tells his patients that three rods lead to Green Zone Lifestyle:

- *The first way is creativity*. Dervish tells his patients to take up a hobby. They should spend their leisure time on an activity that gives them pleasure. When they pursue a hobby, it may gradually become their passion that may turn their dream into reality. One of Dervish's patients became a photographer, a gardener, and yet another took up music.

- *The second way is sharing*. When a patient picks up a hobby and becomes absorbed in it, Dervish tells them to share their hobby with like-minded friends, out of which a congenial group may result. Such forum should be named Family of the Heart.

- *The third way is serving.* Serving humanity makes life worthwhile and meaningful. For example; one of Dervish's the patients helps deliver free meals to the homeless every week and enjoys it. People who embrace the Green Zone Philosophy first enter the Green Zone themselves, then others in their life come into it, and then they all become part of Green Zone Systems. Gradually they begin to play a positive role in their society. Their life turns happy, healthy and peaceful.

When Dervish helps people live a meaningful life, his own life has a sense of purpose. Dervish is not a religious person, but he strongly believes in any act of worship to serve humanity.

O Rabia! Please forgive him for a long letter. A patient is waiting so Dervish seeks permission to leave!

Forty-First Dream

Congratulations to Dervishes on Completing their Forty-Day Meditation

14th June 2018

O foreign Dervish! Heartiest felicitations to us both for successfully completing our forty-day meditation. Our destination is now approaching if nothing untoward occurs.

Rabia read and liked Dervish's Green Zone philosophy. She was pleased to know that Dervish's method of treatment is easy and patient-friendly. The sick person can treat himself without any medication but there is a problem implementing that method in Rabia's Eastern society. Here, no patient considers himself in need of psychiatric treatment. Everyone thinks the other person is a psychopath.

Anyway, Rabia has started with the Green Zone strategy. She is identifying the people and circumstances that can push her into the Red Zone. She has started to pay attention.

Earlier on, Rabia learned from her observations and experiences that every individual radiates some waves. These waves affect the people around them. If Rabia feels she is getting restless in the presence of a certain person, she goes away quietly to avoid entering the Yellow or Red Zone. That implies that the frequency of waves does not match. Rabia thinks that if the frequency of both waves matches, the positive signals are received on both sides. These signals provide cool, soothing energy as though you were in a moonlit night. On the contrary if the feeling is opposite, you feel angry, perturbed and restless. Rabia feels that the people who are friendly, true and loving radiate serene waves, and the ones with negative thinking and attitudes send out negative waves.

Now Rabia reverts to the previous topic, the subject of marriage.

Rabia recalls that around twelve years ago she asked Mansura Ahmed, "Why you did not marry?" She replied, "It did not happen." Rabia was surprised at the answer because apparently there was no short-coming with Mansura that could prevent a marriage. She has beauty, youth, wealth and popularity. Any sane person would love to propose to such lady. She remained perplexed. Rabia can now understand the philosophy behind: "It did not happen." A poet has explained it in a verse:

> *None saw me as the right person*
>
> *I too did not find the right person.*

Rabia is of the view that to find a match, matching frequencies are must. Otherwise couples cannot result. If something is to happen it will happen against all odds. But if something is not bound to happen, it cannot take place despite hundreds of efforts. Whoever understands this phenomenon will not blame another. Whoever does not understand it puts the blame on others.

Complying with her parents' wishes, Rabia consented to so many un-matching proposals, quite different in frequency and culture. But unfortunately or fortunately she was rejected by the proposing parties. They made interesting excuses, for example "The girl is not beautiful." Or, "Despite being highly educated, why is she still jobless?" Or, "The girl is the only sister of so many brothers. What dowry should we expect?" Or, "If her brothers help us to set up a business, we shall not ask for a dowry." So on and so forth....

But Rabia was not hurt by any of the refusals, as she was aware of the prevailing social fabric, attitudes and materialistic greed in her society. Rabia was never so traditional either. So, she thanked the circumstances that resulted in her escape from some big disaster. As Dervish has also mentioned in one of his letters, in Eastern society marriage is a package deal that constitutes a variety of benefits. The worst part of marriage is that a wife is a free sex doll, rather a sex toy. She has two roles that she must silently perform: serve as a maid all day long and become a tired sex partner during the night. Our religion does not demand from her any physical labor nor is she supposed to earn a livelihood for the family. But this aspect is neglected. However, religion's other injunction that says: "A wife has to obey her husband at all costs" is exploited to husband's advantage. Her natural needs of sleep, rest and refresh are cruelly neglected. It is natural that a tired person can neither look after her children properly nor perform in bed in an expected manner. A mother's moods, psyche and restlessness are often transferred to her children. It goes further into the next generation.

Renowned novel writer Amarta Preetam wrote: "Man has learnt to sleep with a woman but has not learnt how to stay awake with her." Rabia disagrees with the writer. She thinks that a man has not even learnt to sleep with her as he attacks her like a beast. He wants to subdue her. A man doesn't know that a woman moves slowly and gradually to sex through romance and foreplay. She hates hasty sex. Again, it is the Action-Reaction formula. A woman responds or gives her Reaction to man nine months later. A man is Action, a woman Reaction. A woman's entire psyche rests on this point.

Another regrettable aspect of the spousal relationship is that a husband adores every woman other than his wife. He has never considered her a life partner – he considers her a sex partner. She is seen as a useful part of the home and children. In this way, both partners are losers and remain so all their lives.

A woman is shy; she doesn't reveal her husband's extramarital affairs to others. Once Rabia had an opportunity to work with an NGO. The project focused on Mothers' and Child Health. During the project, Rabia interviewed numerous women. She learned that a man whether rural or urban has no idea how to live with a woman. He knows only two women: His mother and a sex worker. All other women than these two have no worth for an Eastern man. He can keep them but cannot keep up with them. {Rabia's speculation}

Educated or uneducated, all women have a similar psyche. A woman desires that her partner should talk to her, share her problems, feel her emotions, remember her birthdays, keep his body clean, and talk softly to her. That is her romance. The rest follows in due course. But generally the man does not understand her needs. He just assaults at her. He does not wait for a woman to become aroused for sex. Therefore, most time he does not receive a willing response. This is woman's reaction.

Life is not made beautiful through large achievements; it is rather about small kindnesses and care that make a happy life. It is about caring and sharing.

Rabia was a young girl when she read a book of the stories of Prophet Muhammad's (PBUH) love for his wives Khadija and Ayesha. Then she read the story of Zulekha's crush on Prophet Yousef. Rabia remained mesmerized for years. How can an elderly women or wife attract a young man or husband? How can she keep him glued to her?

Consistency reaps reward, be it in love, the seeking of knowledge or hard work. At times we think we have failed in our endeavors but the results of toil, sweat and labor pile up somewhere and comes back in another wonderful form. The love affair of an older woman with a young husband was revealed in a meeting. It answered Rabia's all questions. When there is an attraction and the man happens to be younger than the woman an element of kindness prevails between the couple. Every man needs mothering. He gets it from an elder woman. There is no ego between them. Love prevails and strengthens the relationship. If the man is older this may not be possible. In this Rabia found the answer to her long awaiting question.

The letter has become long but Rabia has more to say. However, dawn is breaking here. The cell phone too needs to rest as it remains awake with Rabia. Suffice it to say, "Who would have married a curious, crazy keen observer like Rabia? Who could live with all this insanity?" So today, Rabia can say that even though Rabia had little control on the steering of life, the accident of marriage was evaded.

Rabia recalls her senior writers, Bushra Rehman and Neelam Bashir Ahmed Bashir saying after her inflammatory speech in a seminar, "Whatever you have just said against men is simply due to your youth. In fact, the man of our society is coward."

Rabia now understands what they meant. They were experienced and learned women. They meant that winning over a woman in bedroom is not bravery. It is a momentary affair.

Rabia begs leave of Dervish. Goodnight Dervish. Please someday tell me about those dreams as well that take you to a refreshing sound sleep.

Forty-Second Dream

Death and Dream

15th June 2018

Dervish, a student of psychology presents Adaab to Literature-Adorer Rabia!

Whenever Dervish reads the story of the male-female relationship in Rabia's letters, he gets perturbed for a while. But when he reads about Rabia's courage and clear-sightedness, he feels at ease. Dervish finds Rabia not just a woman but also a metaphor for Eastern women's struggle and a role model for many girls who are apparently traditional but in fact rebellious. They do not give up and never surrender to repressive customs.

Through her experience, observation, study and analysis, inferences drawn by Rabia are food for thought for Dervish. The concept of a kindly love in a marriage of a younger man with an older woman is new for Dervish. "Man is action, woman a reaction." "The woman reciprocates man's gift in nine months" is also new concept for Dervish. He will ponder over these thoughts for quite some time. Dervish has met very few men and women who were as self-confident as Rabia. Dervish wonders whether Rabia encountered people who took her confidence for vanity and arrogance. In the words of Arif:

> *"The insane call Arif a proud man*
>
> *We rather found him an upright man"*

Dervish knows very well by now that Rabia is upright not arrogant but do others around her know it too?

Coming to Rabia's question about the phenomenon of sleep. On reading her question Dervish recalled his meeting with a Saint, Sadhu and *Sufi Sohan Qadri*. When

Dervish asked about his philosophy of death, Qadri replied: "We die and relive every day. Rather, with each breath we die twice and become alive once. When we inhale our breath and pause we are dead for that moment. Similarly, when we exhale and stop for few moments in that state we are dead again, until we inhale again. A day will come when we will inhale, but it won't exhale or vice versa. That will be our last breath. We will die, and people will say: "He breathed his last." Similarly, when we sleep at night we die and when we wake up in the morning we become alive again."

At midnight when Dervish lays his head on his pillow he murmurs to himself:

Today, I read a little.

Today, I wrote a little.

Today, I loved my friends.

Today, I served humanity a little.

Today, I thank those people who favored me.

Today, I forgive those people who hurt me.

I have no regrets in my life.

I have lived a full life.

If I die today, I shall die peacefully.

During this monologue the Goddess of Slumber turns affectionately to Dervish, and takes him into her lap to lead him to the world of dreams. The next morning the same goddess affectionately wakes Dervish, kissing his forehead and eyes. She then hands him the gift of another day. Dervish thinks:

"Live each day as if it were the last day of your life."

His philosophy is: "Be thankful if you get what you wished, be patient if you do not ... "

Dervishes' Inn

Rabia has asked Dervish about his dreams. In Dervish's view, dreams are of two kinds: Conscious dreams with open eyes and subconscious dreams while asleep. Dervish with his open eyes had four conscious dreams:

First, to become a psychotherapist.

Two, to become a writer.

Three, to tour the world.

Four, to befriend many men and women.

Dervish is fortunate that all four dreams became reality. As for subconscious dreams during sleep, the experts have two theories.

Sigmund Freud opined that dreams connect us to our past, whereas Carl Jung suggested that our dreams connect us with our future. Dervish agrees with both. Often, dreams remind us of certain past events and very often they unveil what will happen in our future. It all depends on how much one has developed his subconscious, how wise one has become or how much one has nourished creativity, because art and dreams both relate to the subconscious.

Two years ago, Dervish had an important dream he wishes to share with Rabia. It goes like this: Dervish dreamed that he was visiting his parental home in the East. There he met an elderly man who told him, "You are going to start a new chapter in your life. You will embark upon a new kind of work." Then in the dream Dervish found himself in an open space on the roof of a bus. He felt as if he was leading a caravan because so many people were surrounding and moving along the bus. They were happy with Dervish. Dervish too was pleased with their presence. He felt as if he were leading as well as serving the crowd. He is doing that service like a worship."

The dream proved a milestone in Dervish's life because few months after the vision, he was unexpectedly introduced to Wajahat Masood through a common friend Arif Waqar. Arif advised Dervish to write a column for *Hum Sub*. Dervish has already written more than hundred columns in the said Online Magazine.

Then Dervish with the help of his friend Dr. Baland Iqbal started a TV Program "In Search of Wisdom." They have so far aired over 20 programs. Now Dervish receives letters from across the globe. People appreciate his columns and the program. Innumerable people seek advice from Dervish on their psychological problems through e-mails and Facebook. By responding to their queries and offering them useful advice, Dervish performs a secular worship.

Dervish feels that his dream is turning into reality. He also feels that his meeting with Rabia who lives thousands of miles away was also a part of the interpretation of the same dream. That is why Dervish calls these letters: "Dream Accounts."

O Rabia, who poses, the pointed and prickly questions, this is the whole story of Dervish's thoughts about slumbers and dreams.

Now Dervish needs to leave as he must attend to a few patients, heal their psychological wounds and turn their sufferings into bliss.

Goodbye.

Forty-Third Dream

Upright, Not Arrogant

20th June 2018

After the Eid festivities, Rabia presents Adaab to Dervish!

A person like Rabia considers such festivities a cruel waste of time. But she regards such traditions as part of her culture. Otherwise she will ignore them.

Rabia was pleased to read that all Dervish's all dreams had come true. Now he lives a peaceful life. It is a precious gift of nature. Rabia prays for all to have peace of mind all the time. She knows well the value of satisfaction.

Today, Rabia is sad over the sad demise of Mushtaq Ahmed Yusfi, a great humorist. She believes the writer has not passed away but just stopped writing. When Rabia learned of his terminal illness, she prayed for his recovery. She usually does not pray for a long life as that might add to their misery

Rabia recalls a silent meeting with Yusfi. When she visited Karachi to call on Iqbal Nazr, he took her to his brother Anjum Ayaz's place. Anjum is a painter and his house looks like an art gallery. It was a literary gathering and Mushtaq Sahib was a guest that evening. Rabia found him gracious and smiling. That was first and last meeting of Rabia with the great writer. Although it was a quiet meeting in Creek Vista Apartment in DHA Phase-IV Karachi, it made a lasting print on Rabia's memory.

People say that Yusfi was neglected by his sons. O Dervish! To be an artist is a killing experience. An artist stays his entire life in a state of limbo, as if gasping his last breaths. The people around him too suffer a great deal. If he has a family, he cannot devote time to them. They too grow up and learn to live without him. But a dilemma occurs towards the evening of his life. He feels neglected and lonely. His children and other family members usually abandon him. On the other hand, seclusion and solitude gives birth to creativity. The artist produces masterpieces of creativity for his adorers and readers. An artist is a precious gift of nature. It is a tree that keeps on bearing its fruits even after its demise.

Rabia suddenly recalls Dervish's father. When he turned Sufi, his mother must have suffered because an artist, a Sufi and a dervish have peculiar attributes. His insanity at times is uncontrollable. People around the artist go through an agony. Artists are intensely sensitive people. In fact, they are also sensitive about the people around them who they observe suffering because of their ailments. But both parties find themselves helpless

Rabia felt good reading Dervish's comment about her: "She is upright, not arrogant." It is also true that she is taken as arrogant by most people. But let the time decide about it. Had Dervish not known the traits of dervishes, he too would have considered her arrogant.

Rabia through a perilous march of agony has entered a new plane of life. It is a world full of mysteries. It moves dervishes, wanderers and Sufis. They start to dance in ecstasy. Why does Rabia say this? Because she found Dervish's last (42nd) letter in her peculiar style of writing. Dervish had also talked about Rabia's confidence and wisdom. Rabia is thankful to Dervish for the compliments and confesses that they came to her through heredity.

O Dervish! Here a man-woman friendship is considered a curse. Rabia too is fed up with this taboo. No amount of higher education or self-grooming has made any change in this mindset. Rabia opines that only a mother's grooming and training of her child can effect a change in this. It is social compulsion of a woman in the

East to become liberal on birth of a daughter. But she celebrates the birth of a son. She becomes a traditional thinker, often uttering these phrases: "A man does not complain of pain and agony." "A man does not weep." "A man is ruler over a woman." "Arrogance is man's chief attraction." "A man's honor is never tarnished." "A man never gets old." "A man is independent." "A man is after all a man." So on and so forth. But all these emotional assertions make him everything except a human.

A man should be taken as human. He too cries and needs a shoulder to lean against. He too has weak moments and needs a sincere partner who can understand his problems and help him get back on his feet again to face the rigors of life. A man should be considered and made a human first. Other expectations come next.

Rabia still remembers when she was one of the students of Asghar Nadeem Syed as he taught Short Stories and Novels. While discussing mischievous men he would say "A man always brings his trash to his home." He never spoke that way about women. Rabia now understands the logic.

We groom our daughters with the stick of sin and the carrot of reward. We keep her away from natural desires. We implant into her brain the traditional image of a man who is always superior to her. We fear her rebellion. It is our subconscious fear.

We groom a boy like a hero so that his life will be easy. There is no issue of sin or disgrace for him. If this custom does not end, there will be a silent revolution that will wipe out everything.

History bears witness that whenever oppression reached rock bottom, a leader emerged. He would dominate and rule in the name of justice. But acquiring absolute power and plundering resources would turn into an oppressor himself. The same cycle continues as part of man's psyche and selfish, greedy nature; controlling such weaknesses is the very purpose and climax of human endeavors.

One way to do it is meditation, which can be done only in seclusion. In Asian societies people find hardly any time to sit in solitude. They like to indulge in politics, hatred and rivalries which further enhance the hatreds and malice.

Just as we need a siesta in the afternoon, we need a siestas in life. If you do not take time out for recreation and rest, some disease will do it for you.

The night is getting darker; it too needs a siesta.

Rabia from across the seven seas requests Dervish to tell people to talk to themselves once a while. Rabia too talks to herself as well as to Allah Almighty.

Every human being needs a companion. Rabia found Allah, her invisible best friend who does not abandon her. He does not leave you if you cry; if you say something he hears and replies. He consoles, encourages and brightens you up with the light of hope and peace. Rabia is not alone. There is another Life with her who provides sustained support. He always gives and does not take away. We must remain contented with what we have been granted. Every new award may be better than the previous. This is the beauty of nature and its evolution.

Good morning, O Dervish!

Forty-Fourth Dream

Father's Recovery and Mother's Disease

20th June 2018

Foreigner Dervish from across the seven seas, says Eid Mubarak to Rabia!

Dervish is impressed with how Rabia, being a non-traditional writer, nevertheless fulfills her traditional obligations. Dervish cannot do that even if he wanted to.

Rabia has asked about the effects on his mother when his father became a Sufi.

Well, this is a painful story. Dervish searches for words to describe his agony. This is a situation when words feel embarrassed over their worthlessness. Dervish has told Rabia in a previous letter that he was only ten years old when his forty-year old father suffered a mental breakdown. On recovering from that ailment, he turned into a Sufi. He ate simple food, wore simple dress and started to live a simple life. He resigned from the job of a lecturer and began teaching at a high school at half of his previous salary. He became oblivious to material and worldly things which greatly affected Dervish's mother. His mother paid a heavy price for the paradigm shift that his father brought into her life. As his father started to recover, his mother began to deteriorate. His father climbed towards Heaven, while mother was falling into Hell. Dervish remembers those days when his mother's hands, feet and entire body began to tremble.

A medical specialist declared that she suffered from Thyrotoxicosis, a disease caused due to increased activity of thyroid gland under mental stress. The doctor advised his mother to receive radiotherapy at Lahore. He remembers his mother going to Lahore every month to receive treatment. After the treatment she felt better but it proved temporary.

Dervish still remembers the night when his mother was so weak that she was unable to speak. She was in a coma. Dervish, his sister Amber and his father Abdul Basit sat beside her bed all night. It seemed to them that she was breathing her last. That night was felt longer than a century.

Next day his mother was taken to hospital. The specialist diagnosed Myxedema. Her thyroid gland was functioning below normal due to an overdose of Radiotherapy. After that Dervish's mother took Thyroxin for the rest of her life.

Due to Myxedema she went into a depression. As her mental condition worsened his mother became superstitious. She started to believe that her husband had been under the black magic spells. As time passed her disease turned mysterious. In his short story "Mother Earth is Sad" Dervish has expressed the mysterious disease in following words:

Mother Earth is Sad

I am having sleepless nights

For past few months I have seen

Many doctors, physicians and spiritual sages

One says the illness is in my body

The other says it is in my mind

Yet another suggests it is in my soul

An ailment that has poisoned me from head to toe

I accept that my disease has no name

I know it will never go

It cannot be understood

Dervishes' Inn

It cannot be cured

It infuses into the veins like a ghost

It eats up every hope, joy and wish like a termite

One evening Dervish's Mom told him: "Your Dad has disappointed me. I feel hopeless. He has shattered all my dreams. Now I want you to do all of what your father could not." Dervish suddenly felt as if he was a captive of his mother's golden dreams. Before the death of his mother, Dervish wrote a poem "Aging Eyes." He recited it in a gathering in Canada. Somebody recorded the recitation and without telling Dervish sent it to his mother. On listening to the poem Dervish's mother sobbed and sobbed. Dervish wishes to share the poem with Rabia.

Aging Eyes

The aging eyes of my Mother

Whenever I peered into them

I saw wasteland of dreams

A wilderness a home to thorns

Every wish a dried twig

Years old innocent and pure longings

Withered and faded buds lying all over

The pebbles of hopes scattered all over

The aging eyes of my Mother

Whenever I peered into them

I saw ghosts of the past

Fruitless rigors of generations found lost

Serving the men day and night

My mother washed clothes in winter's cold tap water

She grew callouses on her palms from hard work

In hot summers she lit the fire every day

Perspiring in the heat to make bread

She kept up the tradition of sacrifice

But what is the return on the sacrifice

Heart rending sighs and tears

Unnamed islands of longings

Islands where dwells the seclusion

Unfinished dreams and desperation

Blind love for her children

My mother's blind love

For so many years her love kept me bound

To keep up the bond I drank the poison of migration

The poison turned into nectar that ran in my veins

Now my mother's eyes

Have dust of deprivation

But no thorns of despair

On every crossroad of life

My mother sowed a few seeds of courage

She sang a few songs of affection

This courage and affection produced two buds

One bud is her daughter Amber

Her fragrance has wafted everywhere

The other bud is her poet son

A love gift to humanity

The precious asset of his mother

My mother, you are lucky

Dervishes' Inn

Amid the wasteland of your two eyes

That once housed abandoned dreams

Now flourish two flowers of joy and fulfilled dreams

O, night-vigilant Rabia! Dervish did not realize how short account of his mother's ailment turned into such a long and painful story.

Dervish is now exhausted and takes his leave.

Forty-Fifth Dream

Solar and Lunar Beauties

20th June 2018

O Dervish! Another cloudy morning of life says hello!

The wind whispers that the clouds will shed heavy showers. When? Nobody knows.

The storms scare those who long for safe destinations. But when a person has nothing at stake, there is no fear. Rather, the person becomes a rebellious fighter. The storms do not matter to him. They are nothing more than just the splash of a stone in a calm lake.

Anyway, today Rabia's heart says she should talk about "beauty" despite a few previous topics need further deliberation. It's much easier to talk fiction and philosophy but hard to speak of pain. Such discourse brings agony to both parties.

There is an unknown fault in Rabia's stars today, as she has been sleepless for a day and a night now. Beauty is a great reality of life. However, it appears meaningless at times. Beauty is concurrently bitter, sweet, elegant and trivial. The world is beautiful, so is the Universe. The Creator of the universe claims that he adores beauty, so is the case with his creation – humans. But the irony is that humans have drawn limits on the beauty, whereas beauty is like fragrance – it spreads everywhere.

Rabia too has been the adorer of an invisible beauty. The way the universe has been created, there is magic about it. The more you ponder over it the greater elegance it reveals. Rabia read somewhere the types of beauty: Solar and Lunar. In this world the Prophet Yousef was blessed with the highest beauty. He remains Rabia's first and permanent love. The historians describe Yousef's beauty as Solar Beauty. Solar Beauty radiates heat like the Sun. You cannot view a person for long who radiates Solar Beauty. It distorts your vision. Similarly, you cannot look into the eyes of a person who holds Solar Beauty. He emits heat, light, eloquence and grandeur. Like the Sun, such people end up with seclusion. They do not have many friends and face setbacks in their lives.

Similarly, there are places that are overwhelmed with Solar Beauty. The visitor feels helpless in such an ambience. Man has landed on the Moon but has not succeeded in approaching any solar star. Similarly, you feel helpless in the presence of someone who holds Solar Beauty as the solar energy radiates from that person. The companion feels dissatisfied with the possessor of Solar Beauty so abandons him sooner or later. A Solar person acquires quick success but cannot hold it for long. You would find them complaining about their stars, misfortune and bad luck. However, they achieve little in most aspects of life. The same natural phenomenon occurs with places of Solar Beauty. You feel such attributes in some countries, cities and towns. This characteristic can only be felt, not seen.

On the contrary, there is a Lunar Beauty – cool soft, sweet and absorbing. You can gaze at the Moon for as long as you wish to. It looks always complete, regardless of which quarter it shines. When there is a full Moon the force of its attraction increases. Its beauty can fully be seen and felt. The viewer does not feel helpless. People with Lunar Beauty have less fame but more acceptance. Such people have been mostly successful in their endeavors. Their presence invokes peace and tranquility. Such people radiate soft, calm and low-key energy that gives strength to their surroundings. This may be the reason that many poets and fiction writers have written volumes to portray the beauty of the Moon. Fiction writers too wrote much about Moon. The Moon has also been used as a metaphor in both poetry and prose. Similarly, there are places on this Earth that hold Lunar Beauty. People visit high, silent and cool places to refresh themselves. They shed their anxieties at such places.

To cut a long story short, Solar and Lunar Beauty is present in humans, animals and places alike. The Beauty has been described in a broader sense, not limited to a literal meaning or what is described by poets. Then there is another form of beauty – the beauty of Science, Psychology, Spirituality, Sociology, Nature and the Universe.

Rabia had once asked Dervish: "Do the inner beauties like; conduct, manners and sincerity affect outer beauty?" Dervish is silent about it. Rabia knows that Dervish's silence is always significant. He silently waits for an appropriate moment when an opportunity comes along to break his silence. Rabia is content to wait.

There are certain moments in one's life when one feels helpless before the surroundings. On the other hand, every person passes through times when his or her prayers, hard work, and hopelessness bear unexpected and marvelous fruits. Then that person feels the presence of some unknown Power and embarks upon the search for such an Entity.

Now his or her journey, destiny, purpose, outcome, and the meanings of patience and reward change altogether. Even his/her agony and bliss also take a different shape. The bricks of life now bake in a different kiln of experience. These new bricks are worthy of becoming building blocks of any Taj Mahal, Noor Mahal, Inn, Corridor, roof or floor.

When a life passes out of the kiln of experience it becomes calmer. It does not sound like an empty pot, nor does it immediately react to unpleasant events. Now there is a magical rest. The magic that holds wonders and attractions. Suffice it to say the kiln experience gives birth to yet another form of beauty, the real beauty of life.

With this, Rabia seeks permission to leave, with the promise to resume her previously left-over dream in the next letter.

Be in God's protection, O Dervish!

Forty-Sixth Dream

Beautiful People – Elegant Societies

20th June 2018

Dervish says Salam to Rabia, the holder of difficult and challenging questions.

Dervish always reflects and reviews the questions asked by Rabia in her letters. He thinks about his responses to so that he can include them in future letters. But he is fast realizing that Rabia's letters are not common letters. Rather these are tales of dreams, not only mysterious but also unfinished. So, there we go!

Today Dervish will tell you an unfinished and incomplete tale. Since the day Rabia asked in a letter about the nature of beauty, Dervish has been pondering it. Dervish thinks that there are many facets of beauty: outer beauty, inner beauty, physical beauty, cognitive beauty, beauty of character and social beauty. Dervish would like to explain it with two examples.

When a boy is born in a well-to-do family he is fed milk, fruits and vegetables every day. The boy wears expensive attire to attend school. He looks so handsome. On the contrary, when a girl is born in a poor, downtrodden family, she goes to bed hungry. She has no decent clothes or shoes to wear, and instead of going to school, begs in the streets. She looks sick and ugly. It hurt Dervish to acknowledge that beauty has a deep-rooted relationship with health and wealth. Renowned poet Joan Elia puts it like this:

> *Had she been hunger-ridden*
>
> *She would have looked misshapen*

Prem Chand said, "We need to change the definition of Beauty in Progressive Literature."

O Rabia! Dervish's observation and experience tells him that people who have a lamp of love glowing in their hearts have faces that are bright and charming. On the contrary the people who foster hatred and prejudice in their hearts, their faces slowly become harsh and repulsive.

The bloom and comeliness are about principles, dreams and ideals. In Dervish's view, those societies are beautiful from inside whose government takes responsibility to provide free food, shelter, education and health care to its youth. In these societies the youngsters turn their dreams into reality. Whereas societies lose inner beauty where due to deprivation and poverty, dreams turn into nightmares. Dervish wrote a verse about it:

"Those who look around with wondering gaze at every house

They are the dwellers of an abandoned and roofless house"

Dervish is of the view that Beauty has much to do with Fine Arts. If a person lacks an aesthetic sense he cannot relish beautiful faces, pictures and poverty.

Dervish once read some research on the issue. A renowned psychologist found that children of Grade I possessed 85% creative abilities, whereas by Grade X, the incidence was only 15%. There might be millions of schools that prepare their students to work in offices and factories, out rightly ignoring artistic abilities in the youth. Has Rabia ever wondered why certain societies adore, admire and highly regard their poets, writers and scholars, while others portray their kings, generals and dictators as their heroes? Some societies and people are alluring because of either inner or outer charm. Dervish often thinks that outer beauty might be a mirage. A friend and poet Shahzad Ahmed said:

She might not be as gorgeous as you see

Someday get closer to her and see

Dervishes' Inn

Forty-Seventh Dream

Literary Co-Traveler

21st June 2018

In this letter Dervish wants to thank Rabia. Her letters have opened a new vista for Dervish. He is now able to look into corners of his thoughts, ideas, psyche and life which had not been revealed to him before. This look inside was not possible without exchange of letters with Rabia. These letters are re-introducing Dervish to himself from a new standpoint.

Rabia's questions urged Dervish to review his entire life. He observed that his life from its beginning to end went through three distinct phases.

In the first phase, he strictly followed Tradition. In the second phase, he totally rebelled against Tradition. In this phase, he was consumed with anger, hatred and bitterness. He thought that inhuman traditions and unjust systems can change only through anger. Had Rabia met Dervish in second phase, their friendship would not have been possible, because her mindset, questions and ideals would have triggered Dervish.

In recent years, Dervish has been in the third phase of his life. This is the period of his search for wisdom. This phase is instilling into him patience, perseverance and humbleness. Now he knows that issues in life cannot be resolved through anger, hatred and bitterness. Rather problems are solved through love, compassion and respect. Now he is aware that our rivals are also our distant relations, because all humans are essentially sons of this Mother Earth. Things that made him furious in the past now make him smile. The people and circumstances that were objects of his negative judgments are now acceptable to him. Now instead of indulging in confrontation, he seeks for cooperation. He has understood that:

"Winning hearts is as important as winning arguments."

When Dervish reviews his past, he feels that in the previous phase he lived in the Red Zone of anger, but now he finds himself in his peaceful Green Zone. Dervish has a couplet about it:

> *There is a strange ambience of peace,*
>
> *Where I dwell*
>
> *This is Cave Hira of 'Self',*
>
> *There I dwell.*

Slowly, the secrets of connectivity between calm, solitude and wisdom have been revealed to Dervish. About this state too Dervish has written another couplet:

> *When it flew as a river it was tumult*
>
> *As it met with the sea, has gone silent*

Dervish's journey has been a change from breakdown to breakthrough. Dervish believes that every genuine Poet, Writer, Saint, Sadhu, artist, philosopher and scholar scales this journey. This journey tells him that destruction is first step towards construction. Some cannot go beyond the first step. Only a successful artist can break the shackles of old traditions and suffuse his life and art with a new one.

Every nation has two groups of people: A Traditional Majority following the highway of tradition and a Creative Minority moving onto the trail of the heart. The second group's trail turns into a highway over time. The cursed ones of generation become the honorable of the next. In the beginning Dervish was happy about having Rabia as his friend; now he feels proud that both have become Creative Co-travelers. If these dream-letters are ever published and the names of two literary friends find a place on the title page of the book, it would be a memorable day for Dervish. His literary dream would have become reality.

If a student of psychology or literature ever asked Dervish, "How did two writers without a single meeting, write 50 letters and 50,000 words? What is the mystery behind it?," Dervish would reply: "This is a milestone of sincerity, compassion and creativity in the search of wisdom, where "not-being" is "being" and "being" is precisely "not-being." Dervish is once again thankful to Rabia that she became his co-traveler without have ever met him.

Dervish also takes his leave of Rabia because today is the 21st of June, the longest day and shortest night of the year. Rabia should be happy that from now on and till the 21st of December nights will be longer enough for her creative flights.

Forty-Eighth Dream

Mirror of Heart

22nd June 2018

Rabia from a serene valley of night says Salaam to Dervish.

Rabia admits with a heavy heart that shallow societies like hers do not portray artists as their heroes, because they consist of people with suppressed and narcissistic minds. Their heroes are generals, bureaucrats and dictators. Rabia seeks Dervish's forgiveness for having to asked painful questions about the lives of his father and mother. But she felt it necessary. To do surgery, a surgeon must operate on certain parts of patient's body to cure the disease. Soon the patient feels better, and both feel very happy. The disease is gone. Only the scars of surgery remain.

We talk of the mystery concealed in what happened to Dervish's parents. His father's psychological crisis changed his life. It was all unintentional. This change caused a difficult turn in his mother's life, a "reaction", but again unintentional. This "Action and Reaction" phenomenon made Dervish what he is today. The turbulence produced a writer, poet, psychotherapist and Dervish. After losing hope because of her husband's illness, Dervish's mother urged him to excel in life.

Rabia was watching Qasim Ali Shah's video clip, "Saint Maker" the other day. Rabia was stunned for a while. The topic attracted her attention. Shah said: "'Saint Maker' has a higher rank than that of Saint. The Love and Fragrance cannot be concealed. Wasif Ali Wasif says: "Dervish's highest obligation is to conceal his position." Many times, God does help him or her to conceal his or her status. On other occasions the saint-maker prays to God to do things for him. A common man hides his love-affairs. Why not to hide the True Love? Such a person is quite different. When you meet him, he takes you out of Time and Space.

On the same topic, there is a story about another great Saint, Fareed Uddin Attar. As he was busy selling provisions at his shop, a beggar appeared there and begged for food. Attar said: "Go away, I do not have time for you." The beggar said: "How do you wish to die?" Attar replied: "In the manner you would." The beggar lay on ground and chanted: *"We are meant for God and shall one day return to Him."* He breathed his last there and then.

The incident changed Fareed Uddin Attar's life. The saints are of three kinds. Bullay Shah and Shah Rukne Alam are in first category. Many times sainthood is activated by an accident, as what happened with Fareed din Attar. The third kind is where a potential saint needs a mentor to take out his sainthood. It is not possible that one stays as mentee with a Saint and doesn't acquire the sainthood. The connection and love with a Sufi turn his pupil into the same. Leading an honest life in today's world is no less a meditation. When you come across the illiterate of illiterates, you value education, just like only darkness tells the value of light.

Qasim Ali Shah's lecture directed Rabia's attention towards Saint Makers. Many stubborn came before her eye of vision.

This world is full of incidents and events that connect to each other, but you need an inner eye to observe and relate. For that a different kind of homework is required. Dervish's father's condition turned him into a Sufi. In reaction his mother diverted Dervish from his father's path and to the service of humanity. A woman is always greatly affected by any major change in the behavior of her life partner. Nature has bestowed onto her a greater ability to absorb and sacrifice. What Rabia calls the nine-month reaction of a woman is about giving birth to a child. This is the reaction of a momentary action of mating. She absorbs a tiny drop of sperm into her womb and in reaction grows a living organism, indeed, a whole world. This formula applies to her entire life; she produces a delayed expression. She is slow in feelings and slower in sentiments. Her process is naturally slow, yet it is far greater and more complete. This might have been the reason that no woman has ever claimed to be a Messenger or a Prophet. These designations demand a hasty action. Man believes in speed. If he has any worldly power, he considers himself a God. This trend often leads men to psychological disorders later in their lives.

Such ailments are comparatively fewer in older women. Rabia has arrived at another conclusion today. The insanity that Dervish avoided earlier in his life has now caught him. It was in his genes. Apparently, he looks like a secular Dervish, but he follows his father's Sufism. He fulfilled the pledge made to his mother but could not get away from effect of his father's heredity. Otherwise neither would he have become a psychotherapist, nor would he have committed himself to changing people's line of thinking through his precious writings.

He did not rebel to alter his name nor did he adopt a profession harmful to humanity. He could have indulged in drug trafficking or become victim in the hands of those who carry out destruction through acts of terror. A Sufi's son became a Sufi, but the genes too took their course.

Rabia has once again crossed some lines but her flight of thoughts carries a payload that must be dropped when the going gets tough. The thoughts of a writer are a sacred which must be returned to the owner, the reader. Not returning it makes a writer restless, which can lead to some disorder.

Dervishes' Inn

O Dervish! Rabia read Dervish's "concept of beauty" that was based on some bitter realities of life. Rabia can't disagree. It was like a universal truth. Rabia recalls anecdote about a universal truth.

While in First Year of her Masters, one day her pride in having read a few books on philosophy took her to Doctor Khursheed Rizvi. In view of her little bit of knowledge, she threw a plain and bookish question at Doctor Sahib: "Sir! Do you see a similarity in *Nahjul-Blagha* (A book authored by great Sufi Ali Hajweri) and Shakespeare's theories? Do you think he learnt from it?" Doctor Sahib replied in a cool and calm accent: "Look, Beta! Universal truths do not change. What you call similarities, are in fact constant realities of the Universe." From that day on Rabia relates everything and every behavior to universal truths. So there is no disagreement about Dervish's definition of Beauty. Dervish has in a way answered Rabia's question about Invisible Beauty.

In this letter Dervish has answered it by saying: "Positive thinking in a person makes him beautiful while negative attitudes can turn him ugly." On the other hand, Rabia has observed in her life that; youth comes to everyone and it's a blind era. But as people age few lose their vanity; whereas few turn to glow like a diamond. Rabia considers it an outcome of their whole-hearted struggle in life and right intensions followed by right actions. When Rabia refers to waves, she means that inner essence which affects outer beauty, especially the face. That is the reason that without communicating with someone verbally, we can tell that so and so seems a harsh, a gentle, an honest, a liar or a cunning person. You may call it face reading. Rabia relates it to her theory of waves emitting from inner intentions. Sometimes, the inner activity becomes visible on the outer surface, and the person himself does not realize it. Rabia made some observations of older-people. She describes it as the mirror of heart, the mirror of thought, the mirror of intentions and the mirror of actions.

In many cases Rabia was perplexed as the face told a different story than the real conduct of a person. In the end she concluded that "Outer" was hiding something concealed in the "Inner." Therefore, Rabia does not entirely believe that outer beauty could be a mirage. Above all, Rabia concluded that a person's eyes never tell a lie. These tell the whole story.

O Dervish! Rabia feels that Dervish while passing through various phases of his life also evolved. Rabia wishes to know how the journey of Dr. Khalid Sohail turns towards the study of humanity.

Now the Caravan of Dervishes is about to camp at Dervishes' Inn. The travelers are exhausted as the travelling was fast and non-stop. It was journey of intuition and climax of humanity, so it was charismatic. Rabia envisages a new journey in offing. The journey of life is not a last journey. It has no destination.

Rabia needs to talk to the pitch-dark night therefore takes her leave from Dervish. She does not know what time it is with Dervish. Here the early morning star is shining and smiling. Smiling at whom? She doesn't know but Rabia had once referred to the star in one of her Afsanas- Short Stories "Seventh Dimension". The lover of this star goes into an ecstasy the moment it appears.

Good morning from the early morning star, O Dervish.

Forty-Ninth Dream

Dervish's Inn

22nd June 2018

Dervish presents himself today to say goodbye to Rabia.

Dervish also requests a few weeks leave from Rabia for two reasons. First, he must prepare for next Episodes of "In Search of wisdom" with his friend Dr. Baland Iqbal. Dervish and Baland Iqbal have done 32 Episodes for this program. The initial 16 episodes were about ancient philosophers which included *Confucius, Lao Tzu, Buddha, Mahaveera, Zartusht, Aristotle, Plato, Socrates and Hippocrates.* The last 7 programs were about *Al Kindi, Al-Razi, Bu Ali Sina, Al-Farabi, Ghazali, Ibne Rushed, Ibne Tamima, Rumi and Allama Iqbal.* If Rabia has the time, she can find "In Search of Wisdom" on YouTube and watch these programs. For the last few weeks these programs could not be aired due to Ramadan and Eid-Ul-Fitr. Now Dervish must prepare for the next 12 episodes. In these we will focus on philosophes and scholars of Europe and North America.

The second reason for asking a short leave is that Dervish wants to read all of the Dream Accounts again. He will reflect upon the letters written in the trance of conscious and subconscious minds. It is quite possible that Dervish will be further enlightened about himself by once again going through the Dream Accounts. The creative friendship with Rabia has taught many things, one being that a creative friendship brings out the best in both parties.

Dervish also requests Rabia to not only read these letters but also write its End-Note. Dervish has another novel idea. We should share the letters with our literary friends. Reading these letters might offer inspiration to writers, poets and scholars to make literary friends and write letters to them. There is a strong possibility that one candle will light many other candles. Dark nights may reveal light, and strengthen the belief in the approaching morning.

Dervish strongly believes that:

"No such night exists over here

With no Sun waiting to rise over there"

When Dervish read Rabia's last letter he found himself in complete agreement with her that he inherited the genes of his father in the make-up of his psyche. Dervish and his father had different paths but aspired to the same destination. His father followed a religious and spiritual path, whereas Dervish took a secular and psychological road. But both had a common goal in mind — Service to Humanity. His father served humanity by being a teacher and professor. Dervish served people by becoming a writer and a doctor. Dervish learnt from his father to respect others opinions — the foundation of any friendship. On that foundation the friendship with Rabia was built.

From his Sufi father and poet uncle, Dervish also learnt that: "If an artist wants to be successful in his life, he should be ready to make certain sacrifices to uphold his ideals and dreams."

Alien in her own land - Rabia! Before leaving Dervish wishes to present his long poem to Rabia. A mid-meeting will occur between Rabia and Dervish through the next letter in a few weeks. A full meeting would take place only if Rabia travelled from the East to the West, stayed with Dervish and read out these dreams to him, or if Dervish, flew from the West to the East and called on Rabia.

At Dervishes' Inn

Spending creative time with writers and artists

Dervish returned thinking that

When migrating birds enter a garden in a new city,

They make nests in those trees

That emits the fragrance of passion and compassion

That might be the reason

When Writers, Poets, Philosophers and Scholars from the world over enter our city

The passion strings of Khizr (Dervish) softly pull them towards his small hut

In the hut they sit around the fireplace and recite their poetry and stories

The next day they move to their next destination

But the aroma of their talks stays with Dervish like the touch of lips on the rims of goblets

Khizr says: "Every artist conceals a baby Dervish inside him

That grows in the nurturing company of other Dervishes

Khizr becomes a bridge between young and aged artists

Between the Eastern artists and the Western artists

His cottage sits at the shore of a lake

The water birds and shady trees make a soothing scene from the window

His cottage is a beacon of light

Where wandering Dervishes find a resort

And the artists a stage to perform

Whenever Dervish visits Dervish's Inn

He recites his fresh poems and tells new tales to other Dervishes

Dervishes' Inn

This nourishes his passion for literary art

He also aspires to write new poems, poetry and stories

He gets an inspiration to vision new dreams

Dervish still remembers an evening

That day many friends from student days had called on him

The friends who had fabricated the palaces of their dreams in their youth

That day they pledged to rebel against every oppression and injustice

Those were the times when all creative minds got together

They recited the poetry of peace and told stories of love and wisdom

But when the student-days passed

All dream places were demolished

The first group of the youth

Submitting to their parents got married

Produced children and tied themselves with the shackles of Tradition

They offered their creativity to the mighty deity of Tradition

They tired themselves in serving their families and children

They had no time left to read poetry, listen to music or go for a walk

Their responsibilities ate their creative abilities like termites.

The second group had wealth on its mind

They started to believe that poets and artists sell dreams

But this materialist world does not wish to buy the dreams

They wish to buy villas and cars

They started to pile up money and gold

Dervishes' Inn

They purchased expensive painting to hang on their walls

They purchased books to showcase in the book shelves and study tables

But never went to meet the painters of the paintings and the authors of the books

The third group wanted fame

Instead of creating marvelous pieces of fine arts

They preferred to be interviewed on TV and Radio

They did not nourish their art

Although they became famous

But only to write cheap columns and novels

How could have they polished people's aesthetic sense?

They had tarnished their own

The fourth group rebelled

But intensely banged against the wall of Tradition

It lost its nerves and became mentally ill

Their crazy behavior took away their art

That evening Dervish felt that Khizr was one of those few

The ones who remain happy with themselves and within themselves

Khizr did not pay heed to fame and wealth

Leaving the highway of Tradition, he kept moving on the trail of the heart

After hard work of a quarter of a century

He was able to create masterpieces of literary art

His creative juices started to flow

He was never given any award for it

But he won the hearts of people

Dervishes' Inn

Innumerable poets, writers, artists and scholars come to meet him

He blows on the burning ashes of creativity in their hearts

He turns their sparks into flames

Gradually Khizr realized that he was lucky

His Dervishes' Inn had become home to many homeless poets and scholars

Fiftieth Dream

A Way to the Heart

27th June 2018

Rabia too sends a final greeting to Dervish.

In the preface of her book *Urdu Afsana Ehd-e-Hazir Mein* [Urdu Short Stories in the Present Era] she wrote last year: "There I go, leaving your literary entrustment with you. I am embarking upon another journey in a new desert. Life is other name for journey." So today ends a sixty days journey across this desert of creativity.

Rabia read Dervish's dream that talked about the phases of his life. She concluded that a special person must pass through these phases to reach the acme of human excellence. A few people spend their entire life in the First Phase. The majority of people evolves and reach the Second Phase and spends the rest of their lives there. Very few make it to the Third Phase. Those in Second Phase often think they are in Third Phase of their life-journey. The litmus test of whether one has achieved the Third Phase is his or her character. This is the innermost beauty of a person that is revealed on the outer surface.

Rabia in one of her letters had talked about the inner and outer beauties. It is that pedestal of humanity where *Shams's "Forty Rules of Love"* turn into deeds. The deeds are forged in the heat of life's sun. It brings serenity like the 'Green Zone' that requires a lot of effort. Only relentless struggle turns a person into a diamond.

Shams Tabriz said, "The path of truth passes through the heart, not the mind." The journey of truth has never stopped, nor will it ever see an end. With this truth Rabia thanks Dervish that she and Dervish have turned a dream into reality after traversing a challenging creative journey.

This manuscript of their creative discourse will endure as evidence of their creative friendship for years to come.

Over here too Rabia's physical manifestation theory of pregnancy reflected in "Action and Reaction" is in your hands.

Fi Aman Illah – [Stay in Allah's protection.]

O Dervish! Rabia is handing over to you our precious literary creation. She is leaving on another perilous march into some new desert of life. As she said before: "Life is another name for journey."

Epilogue

Rabia Al Raba

"North, South, East or West are not significant. Whatever direction you take, your journey must be essentially a journey to Self. On this journey when you move from one place to another, the Universe and what lies beyond, travels with you." **Shams Tabriz- *The Forty Rules of Love***

This was a Century-long journey scribed in Fifty Dreams. We titled it *Dervishes Inn*. These are accounts of a journey from the inner invisible self to outer visible one. It contains observations, studies, analysis and experiences of life. We named these letters "Dream Accounts." This is a living example of a humanistic friendship. These letters answer many awkward questions. These letters also portray that a sincere friendship is above the ordinary man-woman friendship. You call humans superior to all species but do not allow them to transform themselves to become such.

This was Dervish's long-awaited dream, but it was much more than just a dream. There was someone, somewhere, seeking to turn his dream into reality.

The story begins like this. While working on her project of compiling short stories Rabia called Dr. Sohail to request of the writer his story, profile and picture. She never imagined that her long-awaited wish to interview a psychiatrist was being fulfilled. She felt excited to have found so much in one person. Doctor Sahib is a writer, psychiatrist, columnist, critic and Dervish. A discourse ensued between the two that culminated in fifty letters. We call them Dream Accounts. When Rabia was reading *Tazkra Tul Aulia* [Stories of Saints], she came across a few stories that haunted her. Since these stories pertain to the realm of possibilities and impossibilities. Rabia wishes to share them.

One day, as Rabia Basri strolled along the River Euphrates, Hassan Basri suddenly showed up. He spread his prayer-mat on the surface of water and said, "Let us offer our prayers here." "If it is meant to show off people around us, it is better to do it in the air, where we are not visible to the people." Rabia suggested as she unrolled the prayer mat in the air. Then just to console him she pleaded: "Even a fish can do what you did. What I did even a honeybee can but both acts were far away from reality."

Rabia was eager to have a similar dialogue or exchange of views pertaining to honeybees and fish. But her wish had already seen the gallows of impossibility.

The second story goes like this: "Once Hassan Basri spent one whole day and night with Rabia Basri. They talked about Reality, Insight and Divinity. But Hassan Basri wrote, "During that period I never felt even for a moment that I was a man and Rabia a woman. While I was returning from her place I found myself still thirsty and Rabia a passionate and true person."

The third story is even more interesting. Hassan Basri used to deliver his sermon once a week. But he would miss it if Rabia Basri did not attend. The people asked: "Many notables attend your address, yet you do not deliver your speech if an old woman (Rabia Basri) is not present. Why so?" He softly replied, "A huge volume of juice cannot be poured into a goblet". Once during a speech his voice rose due to emotion. He addressed Rabia: "The warmth of your presence excites me." Today, such respect to a woman is scarce to find.

The entire universe is beautiful due to element of contrast. Here too, Rabia and Dervish, despite having contrasting beliefs, created an intuitive story. These letters were not preplanned. This was an incident of unintentional endeavor. It all flowed naturally without tarnishing the originality of thoughts. Nature is another name of the motion of the universe in contrasting ways. Art transforms contrast into beauty. This is the ultimate truth. It has its roots in the depth of people's hearts. The Tree of Truth gives its fruit to the outside world. In a way we may say that: "There is a time for reality to reveal itself. It is called Social Media nowadays. It existed before but has now revealed itself in the world".

It happened with us too. Two writers of different backgrounds meet on the forum of "Ham Sub. One is the son of a Sufi, the other the daughter of secular father. They have completely contrasting societies, education, work hours, journeys and lifestyles, but both know and understand that there is a day attached to the night like thorns with flowers and that laws of nature do not change. Therefore, despite having contrasting journeys, they reached the same destination. At the destination, a garden has come into existence. The garden is called *Dervishes' Inn*. We hand this Garden to you and seek permission to leave. Dervish and Rabia wish to explore a few more dreams and mysteries of this Universe.

Dervishes Meet

A Memoir - Naeem Ashraf

On 16th and 17th Feb 2019, *Lok Virsa* Islamabad organized a 2-day event, "Mother Language Festival — 2019". The event included panel discussions by writers who create poetry and fiction in Urdu, Punjabi, Sindhi, Baluchi, Balti, Pahari, Hindko, Kashmiri and Saraiki. To address one such session on 16 Feb, Dr. Khalid Sohail, a writer, poet and scholar, was invited from Canada. A psychiatrist by profession, Dr. Sohail moved to Canada thirty-five years ago. In Canada, he did advanced courses in psychiatry and specialized the area of psychotherapy. He runs a clinic named "Creative Psychotherapy Clinic" at Whitby, a town 50 km from Toronto. Other than his core competence of psychiatry, Dr. Sohail is the author of over two dozen books on psychology, philosophy, poetry and fiction.

The literary session on "Freedom of Expression." was conducted on the opening day of the festival. Mie Bhagi Hall of Lok Virsa was full with an audience anxious to listen to the panel that included Dr. Sohail. We too were excited to attend the fruitful session. It was followed by a nice cup of tea with his fans in a nearby cafeteria. At my personal request, Dr. Sahib kindly agreed to be our guest for the night 16-17 February. I was introduced to Dr. Sahib by Rabia Al Raba who happens to be my pen friend for the last three years. Inclined towards mysticism, Rabia idealizes Rabia Basri, a mythological character of Islamic history and finds herself in deep love with Prophet Yousef of Abrahamic lineage. She has done a miraculous task of compiling two volumes of a Short Story Encyclopedia titled: *"Urdu Afsana Aehid e Hazir Mein."* Her enormous resolve, hard work and determination have kept me glued to Rabia for all these years. In May last year, Rabia suddenly went out of contact with me. On restoration of the contact, Rabia told that she had been in bliss of creation and a trance of ecstasy for previous two months. She was writing and receiving creative letters with Dr. Sohail, twenty-five each for a total of fifty. I read those. These contain a candid discourse between a secular person and a religious Sufi. Despite having divergent views about life, the secular scholar has beautifully transformed the Sufi-woman into a balanced, passionate and more rational person. This has been achieved through right intent, sincerity and respect. Their letters were compiled into the book. The book named *Dervishon Ka Dera* has been recently published from India and Canada. After reading the letters I was impressed, touched and moved, having behold the clarity of thought, mind and focus of Dr. Sohail. The book has received unprecedented acceptance and readership all over the world.

With this background in mind, I was curiously waiting to personally meet Dr. Sahib during the upcoming Festival in Islamabad. I was lucky to have Dr. Sohail at our place. On night 16/17 February 2019, Muhammad Ilyas, Dr. Sohail and myself had a marathon intellectual session at our home. Muhammad Ilyas is an author of six novels, namely; *Kohar, Barf, Barish, Dhoop, Purwa and Habs*. Besides having written over three hundred Afsanas [short stories] in his ten books. Muhammad Ilyas too is a dervish who is indifferent to any fame or popularity. Every year he is nominated for Pride of Performance but being a non-member of any literary cult, he is denied any recognition. Dr. Sahib proposed that Muhammad Ilyas should participate in the writing of a book containing the correspondence between two Dervishes: Muhammad Ilyas and Khalid Sohail. Muhammad Ilyas agreed to it and we are anxiously waiting to see the book by next year.

The discourse between two Dervishes covered a wide canvas, commencing with the wisdom of ancient, medieval and modern traditions and covering the institution of marriage, love, romance and friendship.

About collective wisdom, Dr. Sohail was of the view that there are four sources of Contemporary Wisdom composed of four historical traditions spread over 500-1500 BC. These are the Chinese Tradition, the Indian Tradition, the Iranian Tradition and the Greek Tradition. The collective wisdom evolved by these traditions, be it religious or non-religious is the common heritage of all humanity. The knowledge, wisdom and research are not exclusive to any one nation, race or civilization.

To my question of how, he manages his clinic as well as the creative work, he replied: "Work does not exhaust you, not doing anything does." He further elaborated that besides attending a good number of patients every day, he devotes reasonable time to creative works. He has made a creative forum of likeminded liberal and secular writers, poets and scholars. He calls them "Family of the Heart." Dr. Sohail calls himself Dervish and invites people from all over the world to join his Family of the Heart. Dr Sohail's worldview on the future of humanity is unique and beautiful: "All humans dwelling on planet Earth should be free of financial worries, be rewarded for their talents, and practice universal love and live a progressive life".

Quoting Buddha, he says:

"Do not accept an idea because it is given by a sacred personality.

Do not accept an idea because it is written in a holy book.

Do not accept an idea because it is accepted by all.

Only accept the idea whispered by your heart.

Your own experience is your best teacher."

He also quotes Buddha / Siddhartha in the famous novel by Herman Hesse: "When the Princess asked Siddhartha what he learnt from many years of meditation and dangerous wanderings, Siddhartha (Gautama Buddha) replied: *"I can fast, I can think, and I can wait."*

About love and relationships, Dr. Sohail has his own conclusions: "There are two types of loves: Shallow love and deep love. Shallow love manifests anger, jealousy, doubts, rivalry and suffering. Deep love offers trust, peace and happiness forever." About love, sex and marriage, Dr. Sohail has a very clear and logical theory. In one of his letters to Rabia, Dr Sohail writes:

"Not everybody knows the value of the bonds of friendship, romance, love and sex. Those who can find, recognize and value these connections are few and special. Rabia is one of them. This is such a pedestal of intellect where human feelings cannot be expressed in words. Dervish cannot hold back from receiving a relevant verse here:

Apparently calm water conceals a strong current underneath

What shows a brief affection, is stronger and everlasting indeed

People with whom Dervish discussed their sex life during his professional and social life, can be divided into three groups. He denotes them with 3R's. The first "R" stands for Reproduction. These are traditional couples who wish to become parents. They use sex to produce children. The second "R" is for Relationship. Couples in this group are in love with each other, however they do not use sex only to produce children. They believe that having sex is a physical manifestation of their love. The third "R" denotes Recreation. These couples are mostly found in the West. To them engaging in a sexual relationship is more of a pleasant pastime, like watching a movie or eating a hamburger. Dervish also met couples who in various phases of their life experimented with various facets of sex. Values and preferences about love, friendship and sex have been changing with the times. Dervish has his own opinion in this regard: "Any adult couple, man-woman, two men or two women, have full right to get into any kind of mutually agreed romantic relationship." Dervish's own voyage of love, romance and sex was quite complex and cumbersome, not narrate-able in few words. He was raised in the East under the thick umbrella of religious and moral values. But when he landed in the West, he endeavored to understand human relations through the perspective of psychology instead of morality. Dervish has always strived to respect women. He has many female friends. Most of them remained his friends throughout his life. A few months ago, one of his old friends left a message to call her. When Dervish called back, she told him that she suffers from terminal cancer and had only a few months to live. She had decided to see her old friends, and Dervish was one of them. When Dervish went to see her, she met him with the same old warmth. Dervish felt so happy to know that the old friend remembered him for so many years. Through his professional and romantic experiences Dervish has arrived at certain findings: "Men and women have different psychology. Many women wish to have romantic discourse before sexual intercourse. Whereas many men want to have sex before embarking upon the journey of romance and love. "While living in the West, Dervish observed that the West has accepted "dating". Most parents urge their young sons or daughters to have multiple friendships. They think this gives them ample opportunity to know their preferences to make an informed and wise decision about their life partners. They don't want their children to marry their "first love". Whereas, the dwellers of the East follow the single-liner of their favorite poet, Faraz:

Ham mohabbat mein bhi Toheed kay qaail hein Faraz...

[O Faraz! In love affairs too, we believe in oneness of beloved...]

Since the East has not yet accepted dating, young people remain unaware of the pleasures of getting to know ones romantic partner before marriage. In the East, friendship, love and sex and children are integral parts of a package called "marriage". Whereas in the West, people can enjoy each of these relations separately.

In the West Dervish met many couples living together without marriage as well as couples who got married but did not have children, and many unmarried mothers. Dervish knows many men and women who remarried after divorcing their first spouse, and whose second marriage was happier than the first. Another pleasant aspect of the West is that people respect others' decisions. Unlike in the East, people in the West pay no heed to what other people think or say. They make decisions using their own judgment and deliberation. The best thing about their decisions is that people take full responsibility. They do not blame God or their relatives for problems."

It was a treat to meet and interact with scholars like Dr. Sohail. I wish I could have spent more time with Dervishes like Dr. Sohail.

Dervishes Inn: Views of Writers and Friends

It is really wonderful for me to read these dream letters. I have heard a lot about Dr. Khalid Sohail from Ameer Hussain Jaffary. Where Rabia is concerned, I know she is a pretty determined and brave girl. These are her personal qualities but as a writer she has made herself acknowledged. This sort of dialogue will create something very new and may be unique.

Salma Awan

*****

An incredible way of putting even controversial thoughts into polite and charming words.

Ashfaq Ahmed

*****

I am overwhelmed by this dialogue. My emotions are so stirred up that I do not know what to say.

Ishrat Popal

*****

Wisdom is the inner light that helps people see in the dark. These are golden words, Sir, and define the inner intellectual self. Thanks so much for sharing this wisdom. Just finished reading your book *Darveshon ka Dera*.

This book is a masterpiece of dialogue between two quite different philosophies. It is also impressive how you accommodate each other's ideas and give space to each other to explore the origin of reality and personal truth. This book builds a bridge between religious and scientific worldviews. It reflects a journey of two seekers of truth.

Abdul Sattar

*****

Dr. Sahab! I just finished the book. I hope both of you write more letters. An excellent experience to read the psychology of spirituality and social issues of two different societies in one book. The letters are full of wisdom and learning. Congratulations on the fulfillment of your dreams. Regards.

Mian Ehsan Javed

******

My dear Sohail,

Reading your new book. I found it extremely thought- provoking, extracting the juices of all the knowledge and wisdom that you have amassed, during your life experiences and through your profound extensive studies. The long dreamy letters bring to the fore human relationships, your views on friendship, your concept of spirituality and physicality, your ideal way of living and finally your deep concern for humanity. While reading the long letters, I found intimate parts of your life and the lives of your acquaintances and as well, sparkles with gems acquired through your in depth study of religions. The lucidity and spontaneity make this book a wonderful read. I wish I could have half your memory. You are so alive here in these exquisite letters and also responsible for many a living friends portrayed in this book. Great going dear friend…..

Zahir Anwar

*****

Dear Rabia!

Senior writer and doctor, Khalid Sohail is my mentor. I was with him in Canada a few weeks back. To improve my Urdu writing he suggested that I read the prose of Rabia Al Raba. He advised that Rabia's diction is beautiful. Reading her work would help me improve my coherence. After I return to Oklahoma, Dr. Sohail sent me a PDF of his and Rabia's letters. The next morning I opened my computer and started to read the book containing their letters. My patients had not yet started to arrive. I thought I should go to the coffee room and get some coffee. I entered the room only to find a Drug Rep waiting for me at the breakfast table. I had no energy to listen to the rhetoric about why their medicines were better than others', so I went back to wait for my patients. There was rush of patients that day, but during the breaks I finished the book. However, I re-read few letters when I returned home. I had already read a few of those letters on the website of HUM SUB.

Rabia! Your writing is beautiful indeed. I hope my Urdu will improve by reading your letters. I also hope you keep writing. In one of the initial letters you wrote that you have been observing life from the window of a self-imposed prison. Here I recall an English movie that I saw many years ago: Tuck Everlasting. Tuck and Vinnie loved each other. Tuck's whole family has drunk an elixir and become eternal. He tells Vinnie: "Don't be scared of death but fear a life that was never lived...." I agree with him. Life is precious because it has been given only once. I am here to learn from you, therefore would avoid advising. But should you keep watching from your prison the life that is dancing outside? On this occasion, I request you to listen to Lien's this song and feel it:

I hope you never lose your sense of wonder

You get your fill to eat but always keep that hunger

Dervishes' Inn

May you never take one single breath for granted

God forbid love ever leave you empty-handed

I hope you still feel small when you stand beside the ocean

Whenever one door closes I hope one more opens

Promise me that you'll give faith a fighting chance

And when you get the choice to sit it out or dance

I hope you dance

I hope you dance

I hope you never fear those mountains in the distance

Never settle for the path of least resistance

Living might mean taking chances, but they're worth taking

Loving might be a mistake, but it's worth making

Don't let some hell-bent heart leave you bitter

When you come close to selling out, reconsider

Give the heavens above more than just a passing glance

And when you get the choice to sit it out or dance

I hope you dance

I hope you dance

Dr. Lubna Mirza

*****

Khalid Sohail's book: Love, Sex and Marriage made me his friend. The book said: "Befriending an eastern woman annoys men related to her". Sure enough that won't happen with me, I extended my hand of friendship towards Khalid Sohail. I also started a dialogue with him to make people believe that a friendship between an eastern woman and a western man was possible. Khalid Sohail has also talked about it in Dervishes' Inn. After moving and living in the West we learnt that friendship, love, sex, marriage and producing children was not a package as we had thought before. It was difficult if not impossible to find all in with person. If a person finds all in one, good enough but the desire of all in one can disturb one's life. If this fact is known and believed by all, any man-woman relationship would be much easier and charming.

In Sohail's words: "Friendship is a cake and romance is an icing." I go a step further to say: "If you own a cake, enjoy it even if you don't find an icing with it."

Zahra Naqvi

*****

A beautiful exchange of thoughts and ideas, radiating the light of knowledge and wisdom.

Fazle Rabbi Raahi

*****

Reflection within Reflection

Dr. Khalid Sohail and Rabia Al Raba are looking for the truth in their respective stories. They must have never imagined, this is how truth would reveal upon the minds of both. Truth is not about materials; brick and clay. It's rather about contentment. Both characters of this story have deep rooted inner ambience and respective societies. Yet they wish to transform the present conditions through confession, reconciliation and genetic engineering.

Beena Goindi

*****

You both are beautiful, so are your letters.

Abdul Ghaffur Chaudhry

*****

www.ingramcontent.com/pod-product-compliance
Lightning Source LLC
Chambersburg PA
CBHW030321020726
47493CB00004B/1109